Just a Bit Bossy

(Straight Guys Book 12)

Alessandra Hazard

Copyright © 2021 Alessandra Hazard

ISBN: 9798455364204

All rights reserved. This book or any portion thereof may not be reproduced or used in any manner whatsoever without the express written permission of the author except for the use of brief quotations in a book review.

This book contains explicit M/M content and graphic language. For mature audiences only.

Table of Contents

Chapter 1 5

Chapter 2 17

Chapter 3 22

Chapter 4 28

Chapter 5 37

Chapter 6 49

Chapter 7 56

Chapter 8 64

Chapter 9 77

Chapter 10 84

Chapter 11 91

Chapter 12 99

Chapter 13 108

Chapter 14 119

Chapter 15 124

Chapter 16 130

Chapter 17 140

Chapter 18 150

Chapter 19 157

Chapter 20 164

Chapter 21 170

Chapter 22 176

Chapter 23 184

Chapter 24 200

Chapter 25 204

Chapter 26 210

Chapter 27 215

Chapter 28 228

Chapter 29 245

About the Author 253

Chapter 1

The day Nate Parrish met his demon of a boss had started inconspicuously enough.

He was just one of the many protesters gathered at the gates of the Caldwell Group's headquarters. The tall building provided some protection from the cold October wind, but that was pretty much the only good thing about the situation. They were being ignored, the security guards simply monitoring them from afar.

"It's useless," someone in the thinning crowd grumbled. "They're not going to come out and actually listen to us. We're wasting our time."

Others were nodding, looking dejected.

Nate frowned and lifted his sign higher. He refused to give up that easily. He wouldn't let this soulless corporation destroy his favorite gaming franchise.

"Come on, guys." Nate stepped forward. "Come on, we just need to be louder," he said, looking at the other guys. There were only sixteen left, which was a little disheartening, but Nate didn't let it show on his face. His dad always said that to make people believe in something you needed to look like you believed in it yourself, and Nate knew it was true. "We can't let those assholes get away with it! Rangers deserve better! For Rangers!"

To his relief, the others seemed to become emboldened enough by his words and started yelling "YEAH, FOR RANGERS" at the top of their lungs.

Grinning, Nate did the same, and soon their shouts started attracting attention. Security guards approached them, demanding that they stop disrupting people's work.

"We won't leave until we are heard!" Nate said. "Tell those greedy assholes on the board to come down and meet us!"

The other guys made approving loud noises, clapping him on the back.

Encouraged, Nate shouted louder, "They won't ignore us! They can't silence us—"

"What's going on here?" said a cold voice.

The hush was instant.

Nate turned—and met piercing black eyes.

He'd never seen black eyes before. He'd seen dark brown on the verge of black but never pitch, true black—outside of TV characters possessed by demons. This man had them: deep black eyes.

It took him a moment to wrench his gaze away and see the man those eyes belonged to.

Tall. Immaculate gray suit hugging the broad shoulders. Dark hair, finely shaped, heavy brows that made his hawk-like gaze rather unsettling. A five o'clock shadow, despite the early hour. There was something distinctly Mediterranean about his looks—Italian or Spanish, maybe Greek. The dimple on his chin was the only thing softening his appearance, but it only served to accentuate the hard, square line of his jaw.

From the way the man held himself, it was obvious he was someone important. He practically reeked of power and money, but Nate didn't recognize him. To be honest, he wasn't well versed in the executives of the Caldwell Group. The Caldwell Group was one of the biggest private companies in the country and its internal structure wasn't known to the public. Nate could only recognize the CEO's face, but that man definitely wasn't him. Besides, Ian Caldwell was in a coma now. Everyone knew that.

"We want to speak to someone from the board of directors of the Caldwell Group," Nate said when everyone else had failed to respond.

The black eyes seemed to bore a hole in him. "And who are 'we'?" the man said, his expression vaguely condescending. "Why should a board member waste their time listening to some hooligans?"

Nate flushed. He looked at the other guys for support, but to his disbelief and annoyance, they were disappearing into the gathered crowd one by one. Fucking cowards.

"We're representing the gaming community," Nate said, even though he was pretty much the only one representing them at this point. He crossed his arms over his chest and glared at the man. "We won't let you turn an iconic gaming franchise into a microtransaction-filled cash grab!"

The man's expression was completely unmoved. "What is he talking about?" he said, still looking at Nate.

Someone behind the man cleared his throat.

"It seems he's talking about the new Rangers game, Mr. Ferrara. It's one of the old intellectual properties that we bought—"

"Ah," the man—Ferrara—said, his lips twisting derisively. "I thought he meant something else when he talked about an 'iconic gaming franchise.' An irrelevant IP no one even remembered until we reinvented it hardly qualifies as such."

Nate's hands clenched from pure rage.

He stepped closer to the asshole and glared up at him, hating that he was two inches shorter, even though he was pretty tall himself. "The Rangers IP is a single-player RPG franchise with twenty years of rich history," he spat out. "And your greedy company turned it into a soulless cash grab of a multiplayer game with dumbed-down mechanics for teenagers! The story of Rangers 5 was so laughably poor and incompetent, it could have been written by a fifteen-year-old—a stoned one."

Ferrara stared at him with a strange expression: as if he were a bug, but a mildly interesting one. "Thanks for the feedback," he said flatly. "I'll pass it to our lead writer. Is that all?"

Nate flushed. "No, it isn't all," he bit out, stepping closer. He glowered at the man, his pulse beating so fast he could actually feel it. His anger was making it hard to put his thoughts into words, and he breathed in deeply—and ended up inhaling the asshole's aftershave or cologne. It smelled good. Classy and masculine. Probably cost a gazillion dollars.

"What your company did to the IP is a travesty," he ground out at last. "If you can't do the IP justice, sell it to a competent developer that will."

The man laughed, his white teeth flashing against his golden skin.

"You hear that, Daniel?" he said, clearly talking to the man behind him, even though his black eyes remained on Nate. "The boy says we should sell the IP to a competent developer."

The man—Daniel—laughed uncertainly, as if he wasn't sure what kind of reaction was expected from him but wanted to please that dick.

It was absolutely sickening.

"If you're surrounded by suck-ups"—Nate sneered at Daniel for a moment before glowering at Ferrara—"it's no wonder you don't know your ass from a hole in the ground."

Daniel made a hissing sound, probably scandalized that Nate dared to speak in such a way to his asshole of a boss, who clearly was some kind of very important person in the company.

The security guards stepped closer, frowning. "Mr. Ferrara, we'll escort the—"

Ferrara lifted his hand and they came to a halt. "Daniel," he said, still looking at Nate. "Have the boy brought to my office."

Nate blinked, confused.

Daniel seemed equally confused. "Mr. Ferrara?" he said hesitantly. "What for?"

"Do I have to explain myself to you?"

Daniel paled. "Of course not, Mr. Ferrara. It will be done, sir." He signaled to the guards and they moved toward Nate just as Ferrara turned and strode toward the building.

Nate frowned at his back, feeling bewildered and pleased in equal measure. Was it possible the dickhead was actually going to hear him out?

***

He was brought to Ferrara's office.

Or, to be exact, to the reception room outside his office. And then Nate was told to wait. Which would have been fine if it hadn't been three hours already.

Nate glared at the golden plaque on the door that seemed to mock him.

Raffaele Ferrara
Executive Vice President.

So apparently that dick was the Caldwell Group's vice president. That explained a lot. A lot. Of course a soulless corporation would have a soulless exec managing it. With every passing hour, his hope that Ferrara actually intended to listen to him had been gradually fading—until it was gone.

"All right, I'm leaving," Nate finally said. He had better things to do with his time than sit in this ridiculously fancy room and wait for hours for an audience with the resident tyrant.

"You can't!" the secretary said. "Mr. Ferrara told you to wait. You will wait."

Nate scoffed and stood up. "I'm going."

The woman—Brenda, if he remembered correctly—sprang to her feet, panic flashing across her face. "You must stay. Please. I'll be the one getting the brunt of his anger if his orders aren't carried out."

Nate sighed and dropped back into his chair. Sometimes being a nice person sucked; it really did. But he didn't want the poor woman to suffer because of him. "Why won't you quit instead of working for that asshole?"

Brenda grimaced and turned back to her computer. "Please don't talk about Mr. Ferrara in that way," she whispered.

Nate rolled his eyes. "Come on, he isn't here. Why are you all so scared of him? He's just a guy."

Brenda shot him a look that reminded Nate of the way his sister looked at adorable but utterly clueless children.

The phone on her desk rang.

From the way her entire body stiffened up, Nate could guess who it was.

She picked it up. "Yes, Mr. Ferrara," she said timidly. "No, sir... Yes, of course, I'll do it right away... The report is done, yes... Of course, sir... They said they'd get it ready by four o'clock... Of course, sir... Yes, sir."

Nate scoffed. He hadn't thought people still addressed their bosses as "sir" in the twenty-first century. It was so weird. He'd had a summer internship at a pretty big company last summer—though not as big as the Caldwell Group, of course—and everyone called the exec by his first name. Not to mention Ferrara was pretty young for his position—he couldn't be much older than thirty, maybe thirty-five at most.

"Yes, Mr. Ferrara... Of course. Yes, he's still waiting for you. Right away, sir." Brenda hung up and exhaled. Then she looked at Nate. "Go. He's waiting for you."

Nate was kind of tempted to make him wait for a change, but he really was sick of waiting and wondering, so he marched into the man's office.

The door clicked shut behind him, cutting off all the sounds from outside the room.

Nate cleared his throat.

Raffaele Ferrara lifted his gaze from his computer. He was leaned back in his chair, his posture seemingly relaxed. He had removed his jacket and rolled up his sleeves, revealing strong forearms corded with thick muscle.

Thick. Powerful. Everything about this man screamed strength and power, from his wide shoulders to the biceps straining his white shirt. His hard face with glinting black eyes just added to the whole unnerving picture.

Nate forced himself not to fidget.

They stared at each other for a long moment.

Finally, Nate couldn't take it anymore. He crossed his arms over his chest. "Well?" he said, breaking the silence first. "What did you want from me? Hurry up."

Ferrara's eyebrows twitched. He was probably surprised Nate wasn't tripping over his own feet to please him, as everyone else did.

Then, Ferrara looked at the sheet of paper in front of him and said, "Nate Parrish, twenty-two years old. Lives with his sister. Bachelor of Science in Computer Science and Game Development, recently graduated from Northeastern University. GPA 3.96. A—"

"What the fuck?" Nate said, more confused than angry. "Did you stalk me?"

Ferrara gave him a flat look. "I don't 'stalk' anyone. I have people who gather information for me."

"You mean you have people who do the stalking for you."

"Sit."

"I'm good, thanks."

"Sit." Ferrara's voice was like a whip.

Nate wasn't proud of himself, but he did as he was told. He didn't know what it was about this man that made it very difficult to disobey him.

"Now what?" Nate grumbled.

Ferrara's heavy gaze made him want to squirm. "You do realize that your behavior today was very unwise, considering your chosen profession?" Although it was a question, there was so little inflection in Ferrara's voice that it seemed like a statement.

Nate tensed up when he realized what Ferrara was implying. "Are you threatening me?"

"I have better things to do with my time than threaten little boys who don't understand how business works."

Nate clenched his fists on his thighs. "Then what is this? Why did you make me wait for three goddamn hours to tell me that?"

Ferrara's expression was dismissive. "You were their ringleader. I removed you to make you stop disrupting people's work. But I didn't intend to make you wait this long. I simply forgot about you—until security sent me a file on you."

Nate spluttered with indignation.
He'd *forgotten* about him? But before he could say anything, the dickhead continued.

"Considering your chosen field of work, antagonizing a major game publisher before you even have a job in the industry is beyond stupid. I'm surprised by your lack of foresight."

Nate's stomach clenched. He'd known that participating in the protest was a little risky if he wanted to work in the gaming industry, but no one knew him yet—he was supposed to be just one of the many protesters. It should have been perfectly safe.

"Or was it supposed to be a job application?" Ferrara said, his voice dry and sardonic. "Then I'll have to turn it down. We aren't interested in hooligans."

Nate flushed. He hadn't actually intended to apply for a job at RD Software, the AAA video game developer and publisher that was a subsidiary of the Caldwell Group—he had wanted to start smaller, at indie studios that allowed more freedom—but now that this dick was implying that his company was too good for Nate, fuck that.

He *burned* to prove him wrong.

He didn't even care that he all but had a job already.

The small independent studio he'd had an interview with yesterday had promised to call him soon—they had seemed really impressed with the platformer he'd developed for the job interview.

But at this moment, looking at Ferrara's dismissive expression, he didn't give a damn about anything besides proving him wrong and then rubbing it into his arrogant face. The asshole thought his company was too good for Nate?

"You know what?" he said, lifting his chin. "Let's make it a job application. This hooligan can make a better game than the incompetents who made Rangers 5."

Ferrara *laughed*. Somehow, even his laugh was dismissive and condescending.

Nate balled his hands into fists. "Something funny?"

"Your ambition would be... admirable if you knew how to behave with your superiors." Ferrara's lips curled. "It's not even the fact that you have little experience in designing games. Your naïve views about game development are what makes you unsuitable for my company. You don't have what it takes to work at a big company like this."

Nate got to his feet, his lips trembling with rage. "Then let's make a bet, shall we? You assign me any job in your company, and if I do my job competently for— for half a year, you admit that you were wrong, remove the microtransactions from Rangers 5, and give me a glowing recommendation letter when the six months are up."

The black eyes stared at him, unreadable. "Why should I make a business decision based on some juvenile bet?"

Nate smiled. "What's the matter? Are you scared to lose the bet, Mr. Ferrara?"

"I don't make bets I know I will win," Ferrara said. "There's nothing interesting about it."

Nate smiled wider. "I think you just know you'll lose it—that I'll prove you wrong."

Although Ferrara's face remained inscrutable, Nate could tell he'd managed to get under his skin. He was good at reading people. This was a man who wasn't used to people talking back to him. A man who likely burned to put him in his place.

Ferrara leaned back and regarded him for a long moment, a glint appearing in his eyes. "This bet of yours is very one-sided. What's in it for me?"

"If I fail, I'll—I'll publicly declare that I was wrong and Rangers 5 is a credit to the franchise."

"You think too highly of yourself if you think your opinion matters to me. It doesn't. The game sold eight million copies at launch. That's all the feedback I need."

Nate's fingernails dug into his palms. God, he had never wanted to punch anyone more.

But he couldn't.

Nate racked his brain, trying to think of something that would seem like an adequate prize for a powerful, rich man who likely had everything he wanted. There was only one thing he could offer.

"A strong launch doesn't mean much if the game doesn't have strong legs," Nate said. "You know the game has been review-bombed recently and now has a very bad rating on Steam and Metacritic, right?"

Although Ferrara didn't acknowledge it, from the way his expression tightened a little, Nate knew he was aware of the issue.

"I'm the moderator of the biggest Rangers community, rangersdeck," Nate said.

"If I lose the bet, I promise that I'll talk the community into removing their bad reviews." The mere idea made him want to puke, but it was the only thing of genuine value that he could offer to this man. Clearly good sales—money—was all the asshole cared about, and it was undeniable that bad reviews did affect the game's sales. Besides, Nate had no intention of losing the bet, so ultimately, it didn't matter.

Ferrara was silent for a while, just studying Nate in a way that made him uneasy.

"Fine," he said at last. "As it happens, my personal assistant was fired yesterday. The position is still available."

Nate opened his mouth and then closed it without saying anything.

Ferrara smiled. It wasn't a nice smile. "You did say *any* job. Second thoughts?"

Nate put on his most nonchalant look. "No. Why would there be?"

Being a PA couldn't be that hard. Right?

Chapter 2

Nate left Ferrara's office, not knowing whether to laugh or cry. Getting a job at the Caldwell Group really hadn't been his goal when he decided to participate in the protest against corporate greed. Getting a job as a personal assistant to an asshole exec of the Caldwell Group was the exact opposite of what he'd wanted. Yet here he was. A PA. To Raffaele Ferrara, executive vice president of the Caldwell Group.

The trip to Human Resources turned out to be surprisingly informative. Olivia was a nice young woman with a lovely smile and eyes. Somehow, in the short time between Nate leaving Ferrara's office and finding the HR department, she already had the contract ready. In any other circumstances, Nate would have flirted with her, but he was too frustrated now.

"Wow, you got it done in ten minutes?" Nate said, skimming over the contract.

Olivia laughed a little. "When you work for a boss like Mr. Ferrara, you learn to be highly efficient. Trust me."

That... didn't sound reassuring at all.

The salary made him feel a little better. Money couldn't buy happiness, but it sure made his life easier; Nate wasn't going to pretend that he didn't care about it. He would work for Ferrara for half a year, prove him wrong, and make a nice financial cushion until he could find a job that really interested him. It was a win-win.

"I thought Caldwell was the boss, not Ferrara," Nate said.

Olivia sighed, a shadow crossing her face. "Mr. Caldwell is still in a coma, and it doesn't look good. But even when he wasn't in a coma, he rarely came to this office. He gives free rein to Mr. Ferrara here at RD Software. Mr. Caldwell doesn't really get involved in the game publishing side of the business. He has absolute trust in Mr. Ferrara—and for a reason."

Nate scrunched up his nose, unsure what to think. Ferrara didn't look very trustworthy to him.

"Anyway, Mr. Ferrara owns thirty-five percent of the Caldwell Group's shares, second only to Mr. Caldwell," Olivia said. "He's our boss, whether Mr. Caldwell is here or not."

Nate suppressed a whistle, as he estimated how much thirty-five percent of a company like the Caldwell Group was worth. The company's market worth was close to twenty billion. No wonder the guy was an arrogant ass.

"I see that you're a game designer," Olivia said, looking at his file. "But you've made a good decision. If you can keep your job for the duration of the contract, anyone in the industry will hire you on the spot."

Nate blinked.

Probably correctly interpreting his confusion, Olivia smiled crookedly. "Mr. Ferrara has a… certain reputation in the industry. If you manage to keep the job of his PA for half a year, you'll prove yourself extremely adaptable in high-stress situations. It will be the best possible recommendation to any prospective employer."

Wow.

Nate laughed. "That doesn't exactly sound very reassuring."

"My mom always says 'forewarned is forearmed,'" Olivia said. "Sign here."

Nate signed the contract, trying not to feel like he'd just sold his soul to the devil.

"Good luck," Olivia said. There was a sympathetic, pitying glint in her eyes, which wasn't reassuring, either.

Nate smiled weakly. "Is he really that bad?"

She just winced and said nothing for a moment before glancing around. "Mr. Ferrara is… difficult to please. I'll be honest with you: his assistants don't stay long. You're his sixth PA this year. And after what happened to Mr. Caldwell, Mr. Ferrara's workload is insane, which means his PA's workload is insane, too. You'll have to travel all the time between Rutledge Enterprises and the two offices of the Caldwell Group. It isn't going to be easy. And that's without taking the boss's difficult character into account."

Nate chuckled. "If that's your idea of a pep talk, it kind of sucks."

Olivia gave him a rueful smile. She seemed to hesitate before lowering her voice and saying, "It's not that he tries to be difficult. I think he just can't help it. He was raised like that."

"He was raised to be a dick?" Nate said doubtfully.

A chuckle tore out of her throat. She glanced around again before murmuring, "Don't let his flawless English fool you. He isn't American. He was raised differently, and his mentality isn't always politically correct, if you get what I mean."

Nate's eyebrows drew together. "Isn't he from Europe?" He didn't subscribe to the notion that the US was more progressive than the rest of the world.

"He is from Italy," Olivia said, giving him a look. "From Sicily."

Nate blinked, utterly confused, before realizing what she must have been hinting at. "Are you actually implying he's part of the Mafia?" he whispered, a laugh bubbling up in his throat. This couldn't possibly be real.

Olivia winced. "No," she said, looking like she already regretted bringing it up. "But there are strong rumors that his family is. They're a very powerful clan—people say they have been practically ruling southern Italy for hundreds of years. So you can probably guess how he grew up. He's used to everyone doing as he says—he takes it for granted and sometimes can get carried away."

Nate stared at her. Great. So not only was his boss possibly a member of the Mafia, he also didn't understand the concept of "no." "Must have been nice to be born with a silver spoon in your mouth."

Olivia shook her head and lowered her voice again. "He's estranged from his family. He moved to the US over a decade ago, and he didn't have much to his name. Everything he has now... He owes everything only to himself and his hard work, not his family."

"You can't know that," Nate said skeptically. "They could be helping him."

Pursing her lips, she shook her head. "His family completely cut him off. No one knows why. But they flat-out refused to pay ransom when Mr. Ferrara was kidnapped a decade ago. It made the news, don't you remember that? He was barely alive by the time he was saved by FBI agents."

Nate shrugged. Now that he thought of it, he vaguely remembered that story, but he hadn't exactly cared about it as a pre-teen. "It doesn't excuse his attitude," he muttered.

"He's a fantastic businessman, just..."

"Just not a good boss," Nate finished for her.

Olivia grimaced a little. "He's... a difficult one." She smiled at him. "It'll be fine. Just a word of advice: don't expect him to have a politically correct mentality. He demands absolute obedience. He expects you to jump when he says jump. Just do everything he says, and you should be fine."

"That's very reassuring," Nate said with a chuckle. "But thanks for the warning. I appreciate it, really."

Blushing, she smiled, looking slightly confused. "I'm not even sure why I told you all of that."

Nate grinned. "It's my face. I've been told I have a very trustworthy face."

He really had been told that, numerous times. People he barely knew often ended up telling him their life stories and problems, whether Nate wanted them or not. He wasn't even sure why. He had the typical all-American good looks: he was a blue-eyed blond, with a firm jaw and nice smile. He knew he was attractive, but there were more attractive guys out there. His ex-girlfriend had once told him he had a "disgustingly kind" face. When he had laughed and said he had no idea what she meant, Silvia smirked and told him that he had the kind of face that made people want to own him, just to have his kindness around—or to corrupt him.

Nate still wasn't sure he was buying that explanation. He highly doubted that Ferrara wanted him as his PA for his kind face. The mere idea was laughable. Even before speaking to Olivia, he'd suspected Ferrara would make his life a living hell just to prove a point, and now he was absolutely sure of it.

Well, too bad. The bastard didn't know Nate at all.

Nate wasn't going to give up, no matter what Ferrara threw at him.

Chapter 3

His first workday wasn't as horrible as Nate had expected. It was worse.

The moment Ferrara walked into the office, he took one look at Nate and said, "What are you wearing?" It was said with such little inflection in his voice that it took Nate a moment to register it as a question.

He looked down at himself and frowned. "A suit?" he said.

Ferrara's lips curled in derision. "I can't have my assistant looking like that. Where did you find it? In a thrift store?"

Nate flushed. "Not all of us can afford multi-thousand-dollar suits. Sir."

The demon's black eyes bored into him, unimpressed. "Go buy a few decent suits and shirts." He glanced at Nate's shoes and sneered. "Shoes, too. My assistant's appearance reflects on me."

"My clothes are perfectly fine," Nate bit out. "I'm not going to waste what little money I have on clothes."

Ferrara's jaw clenched. "Fine. Walk."

Confused, Nate got to his feet. "What?"

His boss said nothing, just laid a heavy hand on Nate's nape, and steered him toward the door unceremoniously, his touch like a brand.

Suppressing the urge to snap that he was perfectly capable of walking by himself, Nate took a deep breath, in and out.

This wasn't him. He *wasn't* this snappish, easily ruffled guy. He was better than that. He should take the high ground and not let Ferrara get to him. He could handle some manhandling. He could handle being bossed around. He could even handle being treated like his opinion on his own clothes didn't matter. He could suck it up and deal with it. Because Olivia was right: even with their little bet aside, this was a great opportunity for his career and future.

It still pissed him off.

Ferrara steered him to the elevator, then through the underground parking lot, his punishing grip still on Nate's nape. Nate felt like a dog being walked by its owner.

At long last, they reached a gorgeous, black four-seater Ferrari.

The driver opened the door as soon as he saw the boss, who shoved Nate into the car and finally released him.

Scowling, Nate rubbed the back of his neck. It still felt like his skin was burning from the phantom touch, crawling with unease. He didn't know why this man made him so… unsettled. Unsettled didn't seem to be the right word, but Nate couldn't think of a better one.

Ferrara dropped a credit card in his lap. "Take him to a clothes store," he told the driver, not even glancing at Nate. "Be fast."

Nate opened his mouth to say just what he thought of that overbearing dick, but Ferrara shut the door unceremoniously and walked away, already talking to someone on his phone.

"Ass," Nate mumbled, leaning back against the seat and looking around the luxurious interior as the car took off. "A Ferrari for a Ferrara. Could he be more self-centered?"

"What store would you like to go to?" the driver said.

Nate looked at the black credit card in his lap and smiled grimly. Fine. Ferrara wanted him to buy *decent* clothes? He would buy some decent clothes.

An hour and $15,465 later, Nate walked into the Caldwell Group's office in his brand new Armani suit, shirt, and shoes, holding the rest of his shopping bags in both hands.

Brenda whistled when she saw him. "Damn. You clean up nice."

Nate gave her a weak smile, his heart pounding as he dropped the shopping bags by his desk. His impulsive decision to piss Ferrara off by spending an outrageous amount of his money had seemed like a great idea an hour ago, but now it just seemed crazy. But Ferrara couldn't possibly fire him for complying with his orders, right? It was malicious compliance, sure, but it *was* compliance. The asshole should have been more specific when he'd ordered him to buy decent clothes. So it was his own damn fault. That should hopefully teach him a lesson not to be such an overbearing dick.

Setting his jaw, Nate strode to Ferrara's office and entered it after a knock. "I'm back," he announced, rather unnecessarily.

Ferrara lifted his gaze from the document in his hands and studied him from head to toe, his face impassive. "You wasted an hour of your workday on something you should have handled before coming to work, so you will stay an extra hour."

And then he returned his gaze to his paperwork.

Nate blinked, utterly bewildered. Had Ferrara not received a notification from his bank yet?

He bit the inside of his cheek, knowing that he should keep his mouth shut, but...

"You aren't mad?" Nate said. "I spent fifteen thousand dollars on my clothes."

Ferrara looked up. "Yes," he said slowly, as if he were talking to a small, stupid child. "On my orders. Why would I be 'mad'?"

Holy shit.

Like, *holy shit*. Nate knew Ferrara must have been very rich, but this inability to comprehend that Nate had spent a stupid amount of his money—exponentially more than he should have—was a reminder that this man was from a completely different world. Fifteen grand didn't even register as a substantial amount of money for him. So much for his attempt to teach the asshole a lesson.

"Eh," Nate said. "Right."

"By the way, take this," Ferrara said, without looking at him. He pulled a phone out of his pocket and put it on the desk.

"What is it?" Nate said, eyeing it with a frown.

"This is my second phone. The one I use for business associates and unimportant acquaintances. From now on, you will be responsible for taking all my calls and deciding which calls deserve my attention and which you should be getting rid of. Don't bother me without a very good reason."

Nate stared at him incredulously. "How am I supposed to know which are which?"

Ferrara finally shifted his black eyes to him, his gaze flat and hard. "You'll learn. Or you're fired."

Right.

Keep your cool. Prove the asshole wrong. Keep the job for six months, get rid of the microtransactions in your favorite franchise, get a recommendation letter, and an excellent opportunity to gloat.

He could do this.

He could.

***

"What is this?" Maya said, her gaze snapping to the shopping bags as soon as Nate returned home.

"Clothes," Nate grumbled, dropping the bags into his sister's lap before falling onto the couch and groaning. He was so tired he felt like he could sleep for a week. And this was just his first day.

His eyes closed, he ignored Maya's gasp of surprise as she opened the bags.

"Wait, how can you even afford this?" his sister said.

"It's basically a work uniform. My dick of a boss says his assistant can't look shabby."

"Dick of a boss?" Maya said with a laugh. "Mine hasn't even bought me a sandwich. Did he seriously buy these clothes for you? As a gift?"

Nate snorted. "I doubt Satan thought about it in those terms. He's a billionaire. It's a drop in the ocean for him. He gave me his credit card and told me to buy clothes. I spent fifteen thousand dollars—I wanted to piss him off so badly, but he didn't even blink! And then he tore me a new one when I made his *coffee* wrong. Can you believe that?"

"Must be nice to be that rich," Maya said with a chuckle. "Still. It's kind of nice of him."

Nate laughed himself sick.

"Nice?" he said when he calmed down a little. "Trust me, he's not nice. I'm convinced he's Satan in disguise. I wanted to punch him probably ten times today and you have no idea how hard it was to restrain myself. Ugh, just thinking about him makes me so mad!"

Maya looked at him carefully, a wrinkle appearing between her brows. "Are you sure your silly bet is worth it? Half a year is a long time if you hate your job and your boss."

Nate looked away, ignoring the sudden pang of doubt. It was too late to backtrack now. Besides, it wasn't a silly bet. Personal benefits aside, it was for a good cause. If Ferrara kept his word and actually removed the pay-to-win microtransactions from Rangers 5, that would be totally worth the pain.

"It's worth it," he said firmly before smiling. "I can do it, don't worry."

He sounded more confident than he felt.

Chapter 4

Four months later

If there was justice in the world, then afterlife existed, and Nate's horrible boss would end up in hell after meeting his unfortunate end. But then again, Raffaele Angelo Ferrara would probably feel right at home there, considering that he was either Satan personified or closely related to him.

Yes, that was right: his boss's middle name was actually Angel, which was hilarious on so many levels Nate had laughed out loud when he'd found out. Then again, Lucifer was technically an angel, so it was probably fitting.

"Schedule," Satan said tersely, drinking his coffee.

Nate looked at his notes. "A meeting with the Quality Control team at 9:10. Then you need to be at Rutledge Enterprises for the board meeting at 10:00. The phone call with Sony's Briar Ryan at 11:00 about the exclusivity deal. Emily Stevens has requested a meeting at 11:30 regarding the crunch concerns—"

"Decline," Ferrara cut in without even looking at him.

Nate glared at him. "The developers are overworked," he ground out. "It's bad for the company, too. Lack of free time and poor work-life balance affect their efficiency and—"

"Next," Satan said. "I'm not in the mood for your self-righteousness."

Nate took a deep, calming breath. "I've finished compiling the report you requested," he said, handing his boss the report he'd barely managed to finish before Ferrara's arrival.

The man opened it and skimmed it with his gaze.

Nate held his breath.

"It's inaccurate and incomplete," said Satan at last in his flat, dismissive voice. "You didn't consider the increased microtransactions revenue we'll get from putting the game on Gamepass. You didn't take into account the extra exposure and word of mouth sales that would offset the loss of Day One revenue. Have the revised version of the report on my desk by ten o'clock." He turned and headed to his office.

"It's already nine, and you gave me two other tasks already." Nate scowled at his back, but at this point he wasn't even surprised.

He was used to it. He was used to his boss's horribleness. To his ridiculous standards and demands. He'd had no choice but to get used to it.

For the past four months, Nate's life had been a living hell. His life consisted of his work and his boss. He hadn't seen his mom in *months*, which totally wasn't normal for him.

Every day, he arrived at the office several hours earlier than he should have, because his workload was so crazy Nate couldn't hope to finish it during work hours. Then, he had to have Ferrara's breakfast ready by Ferrara's arrival. Nate was now an expert at making Cappuccino — because it was the only type of coffee that existed, as far as his dick of a boss was concerned.

After that, Nate was expected to write down and then perform a hundred different tasks, running up and down the building fifty times a day, typing up ridiculously long documents in a ridiculously short time, and traveling between the Caldwell Group subsidiaries and Rutledge Enterprises like a madman. He rarely returned home before eight in the evening, mentally and physically worn out.

Nate was pretty sure it was workplace abuse, except it wasn't like Ferrara had ever forced overtime on him: Nate did everything willingly. Yep, that was right: he did it willingly. Call him insane, but he would be damned if he proved the asshole correct and crumbled under the pressure. He was going to be the best damn assistant Ferrara had ever had—or die trying. Nate was pretty sure everyone in the company thought him insane. He was also pretty sure everyone was right.

And the worst part was, he never got even the smallest hint of praise when he managed to successfully perform the most impossible tasks. Of course not. Praise wasn't a word in Raffaele Ferrara's vocabulary.

Not that he wanted Ferrara's praise or something. Of course not. Nate *hated* him. God, did he hate him. He hated him with everything he was. He hated him to the point that he sometimes literally shook with it, wanting an outlet for that hatred, wanting to dig his fingers into those cold, arrogant black eyes and make him *hurt*.

Nate had never considered himself a violent person. But he'd been forced to revise that opinion ever since he'd started working for Raffaele Ferrara, because he very vividly and very often imagined wrapping his hands around Ferrara's muscular neck and *squeezing—*

The intercom came to life. "My office, Nate," Satan said.

Nate glared at the screen of his computer before marching into the office.

"Is the report ready?" Ferrara said, without looking at him.

Nate ground his teeth. "It has been twenty minutes, sir," he said in the most pleasant voice he could manage. It wasn't very pleasant. "The report is over five thousand words long."

The demon fixed his black eyes on him. "And?"

"The average typing speed of a human is forty words a minute. I can type at seventy words per minute, but it would still take me over seventy minutes to type the report—and that's without taking into account the corrections I'll have to make. Having it ready after twenty minutes is simply not humanly possible. Sir."

Ferrara hummed, eyeing him like one would eye a lab rat.

At times like this, Nate was certain the bastard gave him impossible tasks on purpose, waiting for Nate to explode and say he was giving up. Nate was fucking determined to deny him the satisfaction.

"Fine," Satan said. "Have Brenda finish it up. I have another task for you. Go buy me condoms."

Nate scowled.

"I bought you some last week! You can't seriously be out of them already."

Yep, that was his life now. Had he mentioned that buying condoms for his boss was among his countless duties? Because it was. In the past four months, he'd actually bought twenty times more condoms for Ferrara than he had for himself—which was kind of sad and pathetic, but it wasn't like Nate had time for a personal life now—or any kind of life.

He hadn't been on a date since he started working for Ferrara, and he wasn't really one for one-night stands. Call him old-fashioned, but he liked to get to know the girl before having sex with her.

Also, Nate was half-convinced Ferrara was lying about the condom size. Surely there had to be justice in the world and Ferrara's dick was actually tiny? It just wasn't fair if in addition to his wealth, social status, and looks, Ferrara also had a big dick. But then again, Nate was starting to realize there wasn't justice in the world where his boss was concerned.

Ferrara gave him a steady look. "If you don't believe me, I can make sure you're there next time I use them."

Um.

What?

"That—that won't be necessary," Nate managed at last, blinking. "I believe you—I'm already going!"

There was a barely noticeable change in Ferrara's expression, a cruel, speculative gleam in his eyes. It honestly scared the shit out of Nate. That look spelled trouble. It usually appeared before Ferrara managed to come up with a new way to make his life hell.

Whatever Ferrara was going to say was interrupted by a phone ringtone.

His boss answered.

Nate exhaled and started turning away when the conversation made him pause.

"I understand, but it doesn't mean I like your decision," Ferrara said, his voice slightly different from his usual flat tone.

Nate frowned and turned back.

"I get it," Ferrara said, sighing. "Family is important."

Nate shot him a half-bewildered, half-frustrated look. He preferred thinking of Ferrara as a heartless dickhead, but there were moments like this, when his actions and words didn't quite fit that image.

Ferrara's face hardened, a deep wrinkle appearing between his brows. "No," he said, glancing at Nate. "It's not negotiable. He can manage without someone holding his hand."

The caller's response eased some of the tension in Ferrara's face.

"All right, keep me updated," he said before hanging up and pinching the bridge of his nose.

"What's up?" Nate said, unable to suppress his curiosity.

He expected Ferrara to rebuke him and tell him that it was none of his business, but unexpectedly, he got an actual answer.

"Ian is going to retake his responsibilities as CEO," Ferrara said without looking at him, still radiating annoyance.

Oh.

Nate couldn't say he knew Ian Caldwell well. When he'd started working for Ferrara, the CEO of the Caldwell Group had been in a coma after a car crash.

Although he'd recovered since then, the man still allowed Ferrara to keep running the company, though it had been rumored for a while that Caldwell was due to return to work soon.

But Ferrara didn't look all that happy, which was weird, considering that he and Caldwell seemed to be pretty good friends—as much as two ruthless business sharks could be friends.

"You don't look happy," Nate noted.

Ferrara's lips thinned. "His return to work will basically be in name only. Ian decided he'd take some time off work for his son. The kid has... issues and needs his father."

Nate frowned, not understanding. "Then what's the problem if nothing is changing for you?"

"Ian intends to reinstate Andrew Reyes as the vice president of Rutledge Enterprises. I will only be responsible for the Caldwell Group starting from March."

"And that's a problem why exactly? I know you don't actually enjoy running Rutledge Enterprises. You always look bored out of your mind during the meetings there."

Ferrara shot him a hard look but didn't actually deny it. Nate hid a smile. He was pretty damn proud of how good he'd gotten at reading his horrible boss—he could tell that Ferrara enjoyed running the Caldwell Group more.

"You told Caldwell that something was non-negotiable," Nate said, curious. "What was that about?"

A flicker of annoyance flashed across Ferrara's face. "Nothing."

"You were looking at me when you said that," Nate said, not buying it at all. "Come on, tell me."

Ferrara stared him down.

Any sane person would have backed down.

Clearly Nate wasn't a sane person. Stubbornly, he glared right back.

To his surprise, Ferrara gave in. He *gave in*. "Ian wanted me to give my assistant to Reyes, to help him acclimate to the job after a year of absence—and to make sure the guy doesn't mess up. Reyes was a total wreck until very recently."

Nate blinked. Wait, what? "You refused to give me to Reyes?"

"Not because you're a good PA," Ferrara said, sneering. "You're barely adequate even when you're not being disrespectful. But I refuse to give *my* people to that trainwreck. He'll manage."

Nate stared at him, unsure how to feel about it. He actually liked Andrew Reyes—he seemed like a good guy, exponentially nicer than Ferrara. He definitely wouldn't mind working for him. But on the other hand, it would feel like he had suffered for nothing all these months if he switched to another job now. There were just two months to go until he won the bet. Not to mention that he had no intention of making a career as a PA. He was a game designer, and a pretty damn good one. He was a PA now because he was *Ferrara's*. He had a point to make. A bet to win. A dickhead to take down a peg or two.

"Thanks for asking my opinion," Nate muttered under his breath, turning to the door and leaving quickly before Ferrara could give him more tasks.

The Quality Control guys were already waiting outside the office, looking nervous and pale.

"Is he in a good mood?" one of them whispered.

Nate shrugged. "Could have been worse."

By Ferrara's standards, he was positively in a nice mood this morning.

He walked to his desk and emailed Brenda his half-finished report. "Sorry," he told her as he passed her desk. "He wants it ASAP."

She just sighed, looking resigned. "Where are you going?"

"To buy him condoms," Nate said. "I can't believe this is my life now."

Brenda laughed, her eyes already on the report. "I can't believe you still have the job. I think you're setting a new record. You must have grown on him."

Nate laughed. Grown on him? The mere notion was bizarre.

"He still treats me like a bug under his shoe," he said.

Brenda cocked her head to the side. "Does he? I've noticed that he's softer with you these days."

Nate chuckled. "Trust me, that's not true."

Ha, Ferrara being softer with him. What a ridiculous idea.

"Hmm, I don't know," Brenda said, typing already. "You forgot to iron his shirt yesterday and he didn't fire you. That's pretty soft for him."

"You can't be serious," Nate said with a snort. "He chewed me a new one for that, so he wasn't soft at all. It isn't a fireable offense."

"The PA he had before you was fired for forgetting to bring him coffee," Brenda said.

Nate stared at her. "Are you serious—"

A heavy hand gripped his nape. "If you're quite done gossiping, I need you to take notes," Satan said, turning Nate and giving him a push toward his office.

Nate sighed, not even trying to shrug the touch off. He was used to this. At this point, Nate was a little surprised that his skin didn't have finger-shaped bruises from how many times his boss had manhandled him by his neck. He had become so used to this touch it didn't even register as weird anymore.

He wondered if it was weird.

"What about the condoms?" he said sulkily.

"You'll buy them during your lunch break."

Nate imagined choking Ferrara with his own tie. Vividly. "Fine," he bit out.

Two months. Just two months to go.

Chapter 5

Nate was kind of embarrassed to admit it, but he enjoyed watching Satan work. Ferrara might be an asshole, but he was a very intelligent asshole, with a very sharp mind and equally sharp tongue. He could make grown men piss themselves with one look. It made the most mind-numbing business meetings somewhat entertaining. Nate got a guilty, perverse enjoyment out of watching Ferrara make other people squirm. Maybe because for once he wasn't the one on the receiving end of his boss's ire.

"Is that all?" Ferrara said quietly, his black eyes fixed on the financial manager of Rutledge Enterprises.

The poor man swallowed, so pale he looked gray, a bead of sweat running down his forehead. He glanced at his co-workers helplessly, but they all had their gazes dropped, not wanting to attract the attention of the boss.

"Y-yes," the man stammered. "But if you look at these metrics, you'll see that the project should be—"

"Not good enough," Ferrara said impassively. "Next."

The next unlucky person—a middle-aged, elegant woman—cleared her throat and started talking, her tone betraying her nervousness.

Nate stopped listening, instead choosing to watch the infinitesimal changes in Ferrara's expression.

It was his favorite game during these boring meetings: to guess what his horrible boss was feeling. Impatience, displeasure, and irritation were easy enough to see if one paid attention to the corners of Ferrara's mouth. But there was also something else that day... Tension. Ferrara seemed unusually tense and agitated, his fingers tapping on the armrest and then fiddling with his dark blue tie, his black eyes scanning the room aimlessly. Sometimes they stopped on Nate—like now—and Nate quickly looked down until the danger passed.

But this time Ferrara didn't look away. Nate could feel his gaze on him, heavy and intent, demanding his attention.

Nate stared back. *What?*

Ferrara simply gazed at him for a long moment before looking back at the woman.

Nate twitched, his anxiety spiking. He knew he had developed some kind of unhealthy hyperawareness of everything his asshole of a boss did or thought. That awareness had been born out of necessity—in order to keep his job and not lose the bet, he had learned to be aware of the smallest signs of Ferrara's displeasure so he could anticipate his orders. Not understanding what Satan wanted always put him on edge.

Maybe...

Maybe he was horny. It was a possibility. Nate had noticed that Ferrara tended to become snappish—more snappish—if he hadn't gotten laid in a few days. Ferrara had an enormous appetite for sex, if the amount of condoms he had Nate buy was any indication.

Frowning, Nate tried to remember the last time Ferrara had gotten laid. Zoe-something had managed to wheedle a "date" out of him last Monday.

They had been ridiculously busy since Caldwell had told Ferrara about his plans, with Ferrara wanting to wrap up most of the projects at Rutledge Enterprises before they left. Because of Ferrara's busy schedule, Nate didn't allow any of the women who had called his boss to talk to him. So it had been nine days, unless Ferrara had a woman Nate didn't know about. It was possible, but Nate didn't think it was likely: the dickhead seemed to have an allergy to giving women his personal phone number.

So, nine days. By Ferrara's standards, it was practically an eternity. Normally he got laid every few days at the least.

Relieved that he'd found a probable reason for his boss's tension, Nate relaxed a little. It was a non-issue. Easy to handle.

When the meeting finally ended, Nate silently followed Ferrara out of the conference room, trying to think of how to bring it up. After all, it was a little awkward to ask his employer if he had a case of blue balls.

As soon as the door of Ferrara's office clicked shut behind them, the other man said, "You weren't paying attention during the meeting."

Nate's heart skipped a beat.

He wondered frantically if the meeting was supposed to be about something important. "Was I supposed to?" he said. "All of those meetings are basically the same: you make scathing comments, people shake in their boots, rinse and repeat."

Ferrara cast him an irritated look, shrugging out of his suit jacket. "I should fire you for your insolence."

Nate studied him, but it was hard to tell how serious Ferrara was being. "I'm just making an observation," he said. "Sir."

His hands loosening his tie, Ferrara shot him a look. "You've been working for me for months now. Do I still need to remind you to watch your tone?"

"Apparently," Nate grumbled, opening the closet and looking at the row of pristine, perfectly ironed shirts. White shirt, he decided after a moment.

By the time he turned around, Ferrara had already unbuttoned his pale blue shirt. Shrugging out of it, he dropped it onto the floor.

Nate scowled at it. "I know you're filthy rich, but maybe handle your things with care? Sir," he added hastily at Ferrara's hard look.

He still didn't understand why Ferrara needed to change his shirts at work. Brenda had mentioned that their boss was very sensitive to smells and didn't like even a hint of sweat on his clothes—which was why Nate also kept a change of clothes at work—but it still seemed ridiculous to him.

Nate picked up the discarded shirt and sniffed it. It smelled perfectly nice: of skin and Ferrara's subtle cologne or aftershave—Nate still wasn't sure what it was, but it smelled really good. Way to be picky.

"It smells fine," he said.

Ferrara ignored him.

A ringtone broke the silence.

Nate twitched before realizing it was Ferrara's personal phone.

The other man answered it and said something in Italian.

Nate handed him the fresh shirt, trying not to eye his boss's muscular torso enviously. Man, it just wasn't fair. He wished he had a body that good. Not that Nate didn't have some decent muscles, but Ferrara's muscle definition was just… yeah. Nate glanced enviously at those broad shoulders, thick biceps, well-defined chest and perfect six-pack. Maybe he should hit the gym more often. And go to the beach from time to time, though he could only dream of a warm skin tone like that.

Ferrara shrugged into the offered shirt, but he seemed distracted by the conversation, speaking fast in Italian.

After a moment's hesitation, Nate stepped closer and started buttoning up the shirt, knowing how much Ferrara hated inefficiency.

The man stood still, allowing him to do it, a deep furrow appearing between his brows as he continued his conversation in Italian.

Christ, his privileged upbringing was so obvious at times like this. Ferrara accepted help dressing him without even noticing it, as if it was *normal*. Now Nate understood what Olivia had meant when she said that Ferrara had a different mentality and was raised differently. Power, superiority, and privilege oozed from his every pore. It felt like this man had been born to *be served,* and everyone around him seemed to sense it, submitting to his iron will as if it was only right.

It was utterly disgusting and Nate hated himself a little, but he was no different from others in that regard. These days, Ferrara often didn't even need to give him orders verbally—Nate was doing things for him before being ordered to. It was bizarre and more than a little creepy, to be honest.

He creeped himself out sometimes.

When he was done with the shirt, he paused, watching Ferrara's fingers tuck the shirt into his trousers and tighten his belt.

Stepping closer again, Nate fixed his boss's tie and then stroked it, marveling at its pleasant texture. He used to think that overpaying for brand-name products was stupid, but sometimes expensive stuff was actually really nice.

Then he reached for Ferrara's discarded suit jacket and helped him shrug back into it.

And just in time. Ferrara hung up, his expression vaguely irritated, his broad shoulders tense under the jacket. Yep, definitely a case of blue balls.

"Do you want me to call one of your... girlfriends?" Nate offered.

Black eyes shifted to him. "My girlfriends?"

Nate tried not to fidget. "You know, the women that call you all the time? I don't know what you call them."

"I don't have a girlfriend. Not that it's any of your business."

Nate forced himself to hold his heavy gaze. "I'm just trying to help. You seem tense. Sir. You always act like a dick when you haven't gotten laid in a while."

"I act like a dick," Ferrara repeated slowly, sitting down in his throne-like black chair behind his desk.

Nate looked at him warily. "Notice that I didn't say you were a dick. I said you act like a dick. There's a difference. I didn't call you a dick. So you can't fire me over that."

Ferrara simply regarded him for a moment. "I should fire you right now. I should have fired you months ago. You're the most useless, insolent, disrespectful assistant I've ever had."

Rolling his eyes, Nate smiled.

"You say it all the time, but I have it on good authority that I've lasted longer than any of your previous assistants."

"Only because you would accuse me of purposely setting you up to lose your ridiculous bet if I were to fire you."

Nate laughed a little. "Please. As if you haven't been setting me up to fail."

Ferrara's eyes narrowed. "You're delusional if you think I have nothing better to do with my time—or that you would still be here if I really put my mind to it. I wouldn't even need to fire you. You'd quit yourself."

Clenching his jaw, Nate scoffed and lifted his chin. "Right. There's nothing you can do to make me quit."

A dangerous gleam appeared in Ferrara's dark eyes, something almost amused but with a hard, cruel edge to it.

Nate swallowed, feeling like he might have pushed him too far.

"Shall we test that?" Ferrara said.

Before Nate could begin to process what that was supposed to mean, Ferrara said, "Fine. Send Helen or Bridget a message, tell her I'll be free at seven."

Nate raised his eyebrows.

"Helen or Bridget? You seriously have no preference? That's harsh, even for you."

Ferrara fixed him with an irritated look. "Why would I have? It's just sex. A mutually beneficial arrangement. No one is getting used if all parties have an understanding that it's just sex."

Although Nate didn't agree, he decided to keep his mouth shut. He could see that Ferrara was dangerously close to losing his very limited patience. "Fine," he said slowly, still not really understanding what that had to do with Ferrara testing his resolve to keep the job. "I'll call one of your booty calls and tell her to come to your—which of your apartments?"

"Obviously not the one I live in," Ferrara said, his gaze already on his computer. "And not the other one—the renovations still aren't finished there. She should come to the office."

Right.

A little bewildered, but figuring that Ferrara just intended to leave work as soon as the woman arrived, Nate muttered, "All right."

He left the room, his boss's discarded shirt still clutched in his hand. He scowled at it before dumping it into the laundry hamper and pulling Ferrara's phone out of his pocket.

His scowl deepened as he glared at the contacts before he found a message from someone called "Helen" who described in gross, obscene detail what she would like to do to Ferrara's cock.

God, how was this his life?

Nate sent her a message. *7pm, Rutledge Enterprises.*

When seven o'clock came around, there was the sound of high heels before a stunning blonde appeared by Nate's desk. "Raffaele is waiting for me," she said. "I'm Helen."

Right. The woman who wanted to get her throat wrecked on Ferrara's cock before taking it between her— admittedly fantastic—breasts.

Unable to meet her eyes, Nate nodded and led her into Ferrara's office. "Your—Your seven o'clock is here, sir."

Ferrara didn't even lift his gaze from his computer.

Helen smiled and walked over. "Hey there, handsome." She plopped down on Ferrara's lap and kissed him, her manicured fingers burying in his hair, then running down his chest, and scraping against the bulge under—

Flushing, Nate took a step back, but before he could close the door, a commanding voice stopped him.

"I didn't say you could leave yet."

Confused, Nate stopped and reluctantly looked back.

Black eyes were fixed on him with a strange expression Nate couldn't quite read. "Shut the door and come over here."

Nate could only stare at him in bewilderment but his legs were already moving. Fuck, Ferrara really had him trained well.

"What do you need the boy for, Rafe?" Helen purred teasingly, kissing Ferrara's stubbled jawline and neck.

A flash of annoyance flickered through Ferrara's face at the anglicized nickname, but he didn't stop the woman from kissing and groping him, even though his eyes remained on Nate.

"Come here," he said in a tone that brooked no argument.

Nate approached the desk, a knot of discomfort forming in his stomach. His instincts were screaming that Ferrara was up to something, that he wasn't going to like what his boss would request.

"Undress."

He froze, his eyes going wide. But then he exhaled, realizing that Ferrara was addressing the blonde. Not that it was much of a relief.

He watched numbly as Ferrara lifted Helen and put her on his desk. The woman giggled and started undressing.

Just like that. As if Nate weren't even there.

"Eh," Nate said. "I'll go—I'm going home—"

"You aren't going anywhere yet," Ferrara said, looking at him with those black, creepy eyes.

What?

Nate watched, frozen, as Ferrara started unbuckling his belt before unzipping his suit pants. Oh, fuck. This couldn't be happening. This couldn't be fucking happening.

It was happening. Ferrara was pulling his cock out. His half-hard cock.

Staring at it, Nate had a sudden, hysterical thought that the asshole wasn't lying about the condom size.

"Get me a condom," Ferrara said in a low voice.

Right. A condom. Of course that was why Ferrara wanted him to stay. To get him a condom.

His relief nearly making him dizzy, Nate reached into the desk drawer he'd put the condoms in and retrieved one, hating himself a little for how well Ferrara had him trained by now. "Here," he said, handing it to his boss.

Ferrara didn't take it.

"Put it on," he said.

Nate stared.

He opened his mouth and then closed it.

"What?" he said faintly.

That cruel, amused gleam appeared in Ferrara's eyes again. "You heard me. You're my assistant. Or are you saying you can't *assist* me?"

And Nate finally got what this was about. *If I really put my mind to it, I wouldn't even need to fire you. You'd quit yourself.*

Rage clogged his throat. Nate could only stare at that dickhead in helpless anger.

A small, infuriatingly arrogant smirk touched Ferrara's lips. "It's all right if you can't do it," he said in a soft voice.

Nate glared at him.

Screw him. He was going to fucking *wipe* that smirk off that face.

Nate tore the wrapper with shaking hands and then looked down from Ferrara's hard eyes to his hard cock.

Jesus.

That thing was… it was big and thick, the cockhead very red and fat, with a drop of pre-come glistening at the tip. It was the most obscene thing he'd ever seen, especially considering the fact that Ferrara was immaculately dressed otherwise.

Swallowing, Nate reached down with trembling hands and rolled the condom on.

Or tried to.

His fingers were too clumsy, and it felt like it was his first time trying to put a condom on. To be fair to him, it was the first time he was attempting to put a condom on someone else's cock. Jesus, the thing *pulsed* in his hand. It was so very warm.

His face aflame, Nate finally managed to roll the condom on.

"Done," he said with a relieved smile, lifting his gaze and meeting Ferrara's eyes. "Anything else, sir?"

A muscle jumped in Ferrara's cheek as his jaw tightened.

Nate smiled wider.

"You may go," Satan said tersely, irritation rolling off him in waves.

Nate had never left a room so fast. He had no desire to watch his boss fuck that blonde.

Once outside the room, he breathed out, grinning in triumph.

Ha! He'd fucking *won*.

But his grin faded as something suddenly occurred to him. If there was one thing Nate absolutely knew about his boss, it was that he had the memory of an elephant and an utter inability to admit defeat. He was the definition of a sore loser. Ferrara hated being wrong. Utterly hated it.

Fuck.

Chapter 6

Nate arrived at work the next day with a knot of trepidation in his stomach.

But nothing happened.

Ferrara was his horrible self, but no more than usual. He didn't act any differently. He certainly didn't act like he'd basically dared Nate to put a condom on his cock yesterday—and lost the dare.

After waiting for the other shoe to drop all day, Nate finally relaxed by the time he left the office. His sister was actually home too, and they enjoyed a rare evening out.

Next morning, Nate was in a much better mood as he arrived at the office. Clearly Ferrara had let it go. He had nothing to fear.

He should have known better.

After a meeting with the department heads that ended with a senior producer losing his composure and running out of the room in tears, Nate and Satan were the only ones left in the conference room.

Nate eyed his boss warily. "That was horrible, even by your standards."

Ferrara didn't even glance at him, his gaze still on the documents in front of him.

Frowning, Nate forced himself to stop the boss-watching—he spent way too much time watching Ferrara and obsessing over his moods. Enough.

He pulled his phone out of his pocket just to have something to do.

The silence stretched.

Was it his imagination or was there really a weird sort of tension in the air?

Chewing on his lip, Nate stared unseeingly at his phone. His friend Ben had once told him that after seeing his cold and unapproachable boss with his dick out in a men's room, that made him seem like a human and made it easier to talk to him. It was total bullshit, as far as Nate was concerned. Or maybe seeing Ferrara take a leak would have really humanized him. Maybe holding his dick just had a different effect.

A laugh bubbled in his throat, inappropriate and silly. He swallowed it with some difficulty. "So, are we not going to talk about it?" His voice came out cockier than he had intended.

Slowly, Ferrara lifted his gaze to him. "About what?"

Shrugging, Nate smiled crookedly. "About the fact that you tried to scare me into quitting just to prove a point? Sorry, but your dick isn't that scary. Sir."

Part of him, the part that was still thinking rationally, told him to shut up and to stop playing with fire. But it was too late.

"Is that so?" Ferrara said in a quiet voice, looking at him unblinkingly.

Nate shivered, gripping his phone hard in his hand. "Yep," he said. "You really thought making me put a condom on your cock would scare me?" He chuckled, but it sounded too loud and fake even to his own ears.

Shut up, idiot, he told himself, but he couldn't seem to stop.

Why was he trying to rile his boss up?

His eyes narrowing slightly, Ferrara regarded him for a moment, something contemplative about his expression. It made Nate nervous.

"You were right," Ferrara said, looking at him with an unreadable gaze.

Nate blinked, taken aback and wary. "What about?"

"I did need a fuck."

Nate cleared his throat a little, hoping he didn't look as weirded out as he felt. Hearing the word "fuck" from Ferrara's lips seemed almost obscene. He didn't know why. They were both guys. Guys said the word "fuck" all the time, so often that it lost all meaning. And yet. Hearing it from Ferrara… it was weird.

"Wow, so you actually admit that I was right about something?" Nate said, trying not to show how off-balance he felt.

Ferrara shrugged, leaning back in his chair and loosening his tie a little. His gaze was still fixed on Nate in a manner that made him more nervous by the minute.

"You did have a point: I have a high libido, and I'm less tolerant of idiots when I'm physically frustrated."

Nate looked pointedly at the seat the senior producer had just vacated. "You weren't very tolerant just now. Do you need to get laid again?"

Ferrara smiled a little, but his eyes remained serious and contemplative. "Maybe I do."

Sighing, Nate pulled a face. "Do you want me to message one of your booty calls again?" Fuck, this made him feel like a pimp. How was this his life?

"That may not be necessary."

Blinking, Nate cocked his head in confusion.

"Come here."

Slowly, Nate got to his feet and approached his boss.

Ferrara was watching him carefully, his gaze too neutral not to make Nate wary.

"I've realized that as my assistant, it's your duty to assist me with everything," Ferrara said, and there it was, the devilish, amused glint in his eyes, impossible to hide now. "I don't need to go through the trouble of finding time for meetings with women when I have my assistant right here."

Nate glared at him. Really? So this was how the dickhead decided to punish him for not quitting at the sight of his cock? They were playing chicken again?

"Sometimes it's okay to be wrong, you know," Nate said. "No one can be right all the time, not even you."

Ferrara's gaze remained steady on him. "Get on your knees," he said softly, his eyes very dark and so damn smug Nate wanted to punch him.

No.

There were better ways to wipe that smug expression off Ferrara's face.

The bastard *expected* him to explode. He thought this was something that would finally make Nate angry enough to quit. He didn't actually expect Nate to follow the order. Raffaele Ferrara was straight. He was the straightest man Nate had ever met. He fucked more women in a month than Nate had fucked in his entire life.

The best way to outplay him was to do *exactly* as he said.

"Shouldn't I lock the door first?" Nate said in his most casual tone.

Ferrara stared at him.

Hiding his triumphant smile, Nate locked the door before returning to his boss and dropping to his knees in front of him.

"I hope hands are enough, because I'm not sucking your cock," Nate said, his confident tone probably at odds with the way his fingers were shaking as they unbuckled Ferrara's belt and unzipped his dark pants.

It was just a cock. Nate had a cock too. He could do it. He could.

The baffled expression on Ferrara's normally inscrutable face was the best motivation he could possibly have. It gave him the courage to finally pull his boss's cock out of his pants.

The cock was mostly soft but it quickly hardened as Nate fondled it awkwardly. God, Ferrara really was such a horny son-of-a-bitch.

But fuck, this was the most awkward, strangest thing he had ever done. Nate's face was warm as he fondled and stroked his boss's massive erection. God, the way it looked… A red, fat cock straining out of Ferrara's unzipped fly, a drop of pre-come glistening on the tip… the fact that he could see his own fingers wrapped around that cock… it was all so very surreal and so very real.

Part of him couldn't believe he was really doing it—jacking another man off—jacking *Ferrara* off—but the other part just wanted to make him come. He *wanted* his boss to come. He couldn't deny that holding Ferrara's hard cock gave him a weird kind of rush. A rush of power. He made Ferrara, a straight man, hard. He was making his asshole of a boss feel good, ruining his plan in the process.

Nate lifted his gaze and found Ferrara's eyes closed. He was leaned back in his chair, his body language relaxed. Apparently he'd decided to close his eyes and just enjoy the handjob. He was probably imagining that it was a woman's hand.

The thought was incredibly annoying.

No, he wouldn't let the dickhead forget who was touching his cock.

"Your cock is really big," Nate said lightly. "I kind of thought you were lying about the condom size, but apparently there's no justice in the world—"

"Quiet," Ferrara said, a flicker of irritation crossing his features.

"I'm just saying," he said with a grin. "It feels so massive in my hand, I can't imagine women actually liking having this thing stuffed into them."

A shudder went through Ferrara's body.

"Tighter," he ordered tersely, opening his eyes. "Hold it tighter. Don't you know how to jerk off?"

"Figures that you'd criticize even my jerk-off skills," Nate grumbled, but he did as he was told, squeezing the thick cock in his hand tighter.

Ferrara sighed in annoyance and laid his hand over Nate's, showing him the rhythm he liked.

Nate blushed. There was something about having both of their hands wrapped around Ferrara's cock that was just… so filthy. So wrong.

They stroked it together, fast and hard, the cock becoming slick with pre-come, the wet sound of flesh against flesh getting obscene in the silence of the room. Then Ferrara hissed slightly, pushing up, thrusting, *fucking* Nate's hand, and came.

Nate wasn't sure what it said about him that his first instinct was to catch all the jizz in his hand so that Ferrara's shirt wasn't ruined.

Jesus, Ferrara really had him well trained.

The thought was honestly horrifying.

Quashing his unease, Nate looked up into his boss's dark eyes and said with a smile, "I'm the best damn assistant you've ever had. Excuse me, I need to wash my hands now."

He was still chuckling as he washed his hands in the restroom.

2:0, he thought. *Take it.*

Chapter 7

Nate hadn't exactly expected Ferrara's attitude toward him to soften after Nate had once again won their game of chicken.

He had been right about that. He could practically feel Ferrara's dark mood with his *skin*, but Nate was in too good a mood to care. Having the upper hand over the asshole felt so fucking nice.

Of course it was too good to last.

It was the next evening after the handjob incident. Nate was finished with his work for the day and was more than ready to go home and get a good night's sleep. He only had to tell his boss that he was leaving.

Nate knocked on the door before opening it and sticking his head in. "I'm done. I'm leaving!" He tried to quickly shut the door before Satan could give him another task.

But of course it didn't work.

"Come inside."

Groaning inwardly, Nate did as he was told.

"What?" he said sulkily, stepping into the room and shutting the door with maybe more force than necessary. He was tired, dammit. He had been so busy all day. On top of the million usual tasks, he had been in charge of moving their things back to the Caldwell Group HQ now that they wouldn't be working part-time at Rutledge Enterprises. He was tired. He really was.

When the silence stretched, Nate finally lifted his gaze and scowled when he saw how perfectly put together and full of energy his boss looked. He truly must be the devil, because a mere mortal shouldn't look that way after the day they'd both had.

Ferrara said nothing for a moment, just eyeing him in obvious distaste. "You look like a mess," he said at last. "My assistant can't look like that."

Nate rolled his eyes. "It's nine in the evening and my workday has been over for three hours now. So I *can* look like a mess if I want to. I hope you aren't stopping me from my date with my pillow just because you wanted to comment on my messy appearance."

"I'm too keyed up. Come over here and jerk me off."

Nate stared at him.

Ferrara stared right back, insufferably arrogant, confident, and without a hint of shame.

Nate laughed a little. "Is this now part of my job description?"

"It is, if I say so. If you don't like the job, you can always quit."

Nate scoffed. "You wish," he said before striding over to his boss and kneeling.

***

That was how the whole thing had started. *The thing* being the fact that he now gave Ferrara handjobs every time the dick was up for it—pun intended.

It was both extremely weird and not weird at all. Ferrara didn't act any differently toward him just because Nate *relieved his tension* as part of his job.

Nate didn't delude himself into thinking that the arrangement was more than just a matter of convenience for Ferrara. Now the guy didn't have to go through the inconvenience of meeting with his booty calls if he felt stressed and frustrated at work. Granted, Nate was sure Ferrara was still getting laid on the weekends, but the rest of the week Nate's hand was being put to—very frequent—use. Not that he received as much as a "thank you" for his efforts.

So nope, Satan didn't act any differently toward him.

Nate couldn't say the same about himself. He did feel a little differently now that he intimately knew the shape and the feel of his boss's cock. He didn't hate Ferrara any less, but he wasn't as scared of him. There had simply come a point when he'd realized that Ferrara was just a man, made of flesh and blood, who liked getting his rocks off when he wasn't reducing his employees to tears. Maybe his friend Ben did have a point, after all.

The handjobs had another unexpectedly good side-effect: they made him totally zen at work. As his fifth month at the Caldwell Group came to an end, nothing fazed Nate anymore. He wasn't sure why. Maybe it was because he'd already hit rock bottom and nothing could possibly be more challenging than giving handies to the devil. Or maybe he'd just gotten used to his job—or used to his boss. Either way, Ferrara could give him any amount of ridiculous tasks and they no longer made him break into a panic. A dozen different tasks that contradicted each other? No problem. Nate now knew what tasks to delegate to the secretaries and couriers, and what tasks he had to do himself. It was manageable. Tolerable. His job was surprisingly tolerable. He sometimes actually found himself enjoying the challenge.

"God, I don't know how you do it," Brenda said one afternoon after Satan had dressed down dozens of people at the quarterly meeting. "I'm frankly amazed you're still here. No one has ever stayed this long as his PA."

Nate probably shouldn't have felt pleased hearing that. But hey, it was totally something to be proud of. It required balls of steel and the patience of a saint to put up with Ferrara for so long.

"And the weird thing is, you aren't even polite to him," Brenda said, shaking her head in bewilderment. "He actually lets you talk back."

Nate wrinkled his nose and laughed. "I wouldn't go that far. He only lets me talk back when it amuses him."

From the look on her face, Brenda disagreed. "Seriously, what's your secret?" she said, leaning in. "Please tell me so I can help out the poor guy who will be his PA after you're gone next month!"

Right. He would be gone next month. The thought was... kind of weird.

"There's no secret," Nate said belatedly when he realized that she was still waiting for his answer.

No secret at all, he thought as he walked away. *I just annoy him all the time and touch his cock sometimes.*

Lately, though, "sometimes" meant every day, or even twice a day. Ferrara's libido was ridiculous; it was a good thing Nate was a fast learner and by now knew how to get him off fast. Though Nate was pretty sure his boss demanded his *assistance* so often just to annoy him into quitting.

Too bad it didn't work.

***

"You can't be serious," he said, looking at Ferrara incredulously. "You have a meeting with the Microsoft representative in fifteen minutes."

"That's precisely why it needs to happen now," Ferrara said in a tone of finality, his face expressionless as if he were speaking about the weather. "I'll need a clear head for the meeting. It's too important."

Nate scoffed. "What, you can't think when you're horny?"

Ferrara gave him a look that made it clear how little he thought of Nate's intelligence if Nate really expected that he was going to explain himself to a lowly PA.

"Fine," Nate grumbled, kneeling in front of him and unzipping his boss's pants with practiced ease. "I still don't understand how you can be horny already. I did this yesterday evening."

"Then you can blame only yourself for your subpar effort."

Glaring at him, Nate pulled out Ferrara's already-hard cock and squeezed it tightly, the way Ferrara liked it. It creeped him out how familiar the weight and the feel of that cock was by now. Big. Warm. Pulsing. Obscenely thick. A cock. In his hand.

Licking his lips, Nate tore his gaze away from the thing and started stroking it.

Ferrara was quiet, as usual, his heavy-lidded eyes on Nate's hand working his cock. The bastard didn't close his eyes anymore, but he'd recently taken to watching Nate's hand on his cock, which was slightly unnerving.

Nate looked away before their gazes could accidentally meet. He always felt weird when that happened. Somehow, it was weirder than giving the man a handjob.

Stroke, stroke, stroke.

His wrist started aching soon enough. Almost ten minutes had passed but Ferrara *still* hadn't come.

Nate huffed in frustration. "He'll be here any minute now. The door isn't even locked." Not that anyone would dare enter Satan's office without a knock, but still.

"Then make me come."

Nate scowled. "You think I'm not trying?"

"Try harder," Ferrara said, meeting his gaze, his black eyes glinting.

Nate swallowed, his stomach in knots. "My wrist is tired," he complained.

A strange expression appeared in those eyes. "Then use something else."

It took Nate a few seconds to register the meaning of his words.

He flushed. "I'm not sucking your cock," he hissed. "I'm straight!"

Ferrara shrugged and leaned back in his chair, his posture confident and so very male. "So am I," he said. "So what?"

The *nerve* of him.

Nate could only open and close his mouth wordlessly, absolutely speechless.

There was a knock on the door. "Mr. Robertson from Microsoft is here, sir," Brenda's muffled voice sounded through the door.

Nate jerked his hand away from Ferrara's cock, but the asshole grabbed it and kept it where it was. "Give me a minute," Ferrara called out before shifting his gaze back to Nate and lowering his voice. "Well? Are you going to make a Microsoft representative wait?"

Glowering at him, Nate spluttered in indignation.

A glimmer of amusement appeared in Ferrara's eyes. "You can say no, obviously. I'm not forcing you. You can quit."

"Fuck you. I'm quitting *after* I win the bet in a month, and not a second sooner." Before he could think twice, Nate leaned in and fit his mouth over his boss's erection.

It tasted… nowhere near as bad as Nate had thought it would. Just of salty skin. If he closed his eyes, he could imagine that he had fingers in his mouth, and not another man's cock.

Except he didn't have fingers in his mouth. He had another man's cock in his mouth. A cock. In his mouth. His boss's cock.

His face burning, Nate squeezed his eyes shut and moved his head, trying to take as much of the thing into his mouth as he could.

He failed.

There was just *so much* of it. How the hell did women do it?

Mentally apologizing to every woman who'd ever blown him for not showing enough appreciation for her hard work, Nate tried his damnedest to mimic what his girlfriends had done to him.

"You're terrible at this," Ferrara commented when Nate pulled up for some much-needed air.

Glaring up at him, Nate bit out, "I'm straight. Of course I'm terrible at this. Yours is the first cock I'm trying to suck."

A drop of pre-come appeared on the cockhead. Nate wrinkled his nose but tentatively gave it a small, kittenish lick.

Ferrara groaned and came all over his face. Just like that.

"You—" Nate spluttered, springing to his feet. Opening the desk drawer, he pulled wet wipes out of it and rubbed at his face frantically. "Jesus, this is gross."

His gaze heavy-lidded from his orgasm, Ferrara tucked his cock into his pants and zipped up. And of course he now looked picture-perfect and not at all like he'd just come all over his assistant's face.

Scowling at him fiercely, Nate finished cleaning his face and turned to the door.

"There's still a drop on your nose," came Ferrara's voice from behind him.

Nate flushed and wiped his nose. "I hate you so much," he said with feeling.

"Noted," the bastard said, and was that *amusement* in his voice? "Now go tell Robertson he may come in."

Nate did just that.

"Are you okay, Nate?" Brenda said sympathetically as Robertson disappeared into the office.

Nate flinched, looking at her warily. "What? What do you mean?"

She cocked her head to the side. "You look flushed. Was he hard on you?"

Nate nearly laughed.

He was hard in me, he thought, and for a moment imagined the look on her face if he actually said that.

She would think it was a joke, of course.

Nate would think it was a joke too if someone told him five months ago that he would be willingly sucking Ferrara's cock because his boss needed a "clear head" for a meeting with a Microsoft representative.

God, could his life get any more surreal?

Chapter 8

Nate would like to say his life had changed monumentally after putting a cock in his mouth, but... it didn't. He didn't feel any different. It had been weird at first, but he wasn't really freaking out or traumatized or anything like that. But then again, why would he be? It wasn't sex. Neither of them considered that sex. It was just a convenience thing for Ferrara—and a way to get on Nate's nerves, no doubt—and just another tedious task for Nate, one of the many that were part of his job. It wasn't even the most unpleasant task if he didn't fixate on the weirdness of the fact that he had another man's cock in his mouth—every damn day.

Because it seemed handjobs weren't enough for Satan anymore. The greedy son-of-a-bitch wanted his mouth. Not that Nate didn't get it. He did. He was a guy, too. As a guy, he would always prefer even a mediocre blowjob to a handjob. And Nate didn't flatter himself by thinking that his blowjobs were anything but mediocre. He *had* improved, somewhat—he'd learned how to hold his breath and not choke, and his jaw ached less, because as fucked-up as it sounded, he was getting *used* to this. He was getting used to having a cock in his mouth, fuck.

The taste was all right, too.

Nate hummed around the thick length in his mouth, inhaling deeply with his nose as the cock pushed in and out of him.

Ferrara's hand was buried in his hair, holding him still in such a bossy, proprietary way that it was actually more infuriating and distracting than the cock thrusting into his mouth.

The door wasn't locked once again.

A wave of embarrassment washed over Nate as he imagined someone entering the room without a knock and seeing him on his knees between his boss's legs, having his mouth used. The worst part was, he was pretty sure the bastard wouldn't even bother to stop if anyone were to enter. Ferrara always acted like using Nate's mouth was his *right*, as if he was entitled to it, as if there was nothing embarrassing about it, regardless of their sexualities, and Nate had to admit that kind of attitude rubbed off on him in the worst possible way, making him feel like there was nothing unusual or weird about it.

But there were still times like this, when it hit him how utterly *wrong* this was. In normal circumstances, he would never suck another man's cock, especially where anyone could enter and see them, and yet here he was, doing exactly that. Was it some kind of weird form of Stockholm Syndrome? Had Ferrara brainwashed him into thinking that he must do everything to please his boss?

"Teeth," Ferrara bit out, his grip on Nate's hair tightening.

Covering his teeth better, Nate pushed his thoughts away and focused on sucking cock. Whatever. There was no use freaking out about this. It would be over soon enough. He would be free of this man and the strange effect he had on him in two weeks.

Just two weeks to go.

Nate started bobbing his head faster.

***

"Report."

Nate pulled a blue shirt out of the wardrobe and turned back to his boss. "The Xenos Studios director wants to have a meeting with you regarding the outsourced DLC for Star Forces, preferably today—"

"Put him on Wednesday," Ferrara said, loosening his tie.

"ET Entertainment wants to negotiate a licensing deal for the Rangers IP—"

"No."

The answer pleased Nate. He didn't want a greedy company like ET Entertainment to ruin his favorite franchise even more—they were actually *worse* than the Caldwell Group when it came to microtransactions. "You'll have to tell them yourself. I don't think they'll believe that I'm speaking for you."

Ferrara heaved a sigh but nodded, stretching out his hand, a silent command to give him his work phone.

After finding the right contact, Nate handed the phone to him and then stepped closer. Dropping the new shirt on the desk, Nate resumed where Ferrara had left off.

He listened to the phone conversation with only half an ear, focused on unbuttoning Ferrara's shirt and then slipping it off his wide shoulders. He greedily inhaled a lungful of his boss's scent. Damn, that cologne was so nice, masculine but subtle and nuanced. He wondered how expensive it was. He would have liked to get it for himself if it didn't cost a gazillion dollars.

Setting the shirt aside, Nate was about to reach for the new one when he noticed a familiar tension in Ferrara's body.

A downward glance confirmed it: his boss was half-hard, his cock straining his fly.

He licked his lips.

Oh.

He might as well deal with it before putting on a new shirt.

His fingers were already undoing Ferrara's belt before he even made a conscious decision. Nate pulled the zipper open and knelt at his boss's feet. Ferrara's cock was almost fully hard by the time Nate fished it out of Ferrara's boxer briefs.

Closing his eyes, Nate took the cock into his mouth.

He had to admit there was something oddly entrancing about it: the rhythm of a cock moving inside him, the way his head became empty of all thought. It was kind of hypnotizing, in and out, in and out.

Nate heard someone moan, and it took him a few moments to realize that the sound had come from him.

His eyes snapped open.

Several things registered at once. He was sucking his boss's cock without even being told to. He was half-hard in his pants. *From sucking a cock*. His horrible boss's cock. What the fuck.

He froze, his eyes wide.

Then he released the cock and sprang to his shaky feet. His cheeks burning, he darted out of the room and slammed the door shut behind him. He then wiped at his lips frantically, as if that would wipe away the taste of the cock inside his mouth.

Jesus fucking Christ.

What had he been doing?

"Nate? Something wrong?"

Brenda's voice seemed to be coming from afar.

Nate blinked, staring at her confused face without really seeing it, his mind racing a mile a minute. He almost laughed. *Everything is fine. I was just brainwashed into liking Satan's cock in my mouth.*

"I need to go home," Nate blurted out. "Tell him I have a—a family emergency."

"Okay," she said, glancing at the door behind Nate and wincing a little. "But can't you tell him yourself? He isn't going to be happy. He likes having you at his beck and call at all times."

Yeah, you have no idea.

"He's on the phone," Nate said, already heading for the elevator. "I don't want to interrupt his conversation."

He needed to leave. He needed to leave *now*.

Nate barely remembered how he got back home. Considering his distracted state, it was probably lucky he hadn't managed to get himself killed.

He parked his car—*Ferrara's* car, actually, a beautiful Mercedes his boss let him use to get around the city to perform countless tasks for him. Nate scowled at the car, realizing with a sinking feeling how thoroughly Raffaele Ferrara dominated all aspects of his life by now.

His sister was home already, making dinner.

She looked at him curiously the moment he walked in. "Something wrong? Why are you so early? I don't think I've seen you home before eight in months."

Nate opened his mouth, but the lie that was on the tip of his tongue didn't come out. Why not tell the truth, really? Who could he talk to if not his sister? He honestly felt like he would explode if he didn't talk to someone about the utter fuckery his life had become. Pun intended.

"I've been sucking my boss's cock for the past few weeks."

Maya blinked slowly.

"Is that... is that a joke?" she said at last, her blue eyes wide.

Chuckling, Nate plopped down in the armchair. "I wish."

"Wait... I thought you hated him. And aren't you straight?"

"I do. I am."

Silence.

Then, Maya exploded. "I'll fucking—! We need to—we need to tell the police, or—"

"He didn't force me, Maya," Nate said, without meeting her eyes.

He smiled crookedly. "He didn't need to. It was just some weird game of chicken that got out of hand." He chuckled again, studying his hands. "I'm honestly not sure how it happened. I know it makes no sense. It's just... When he's around, it's like my brain turns off and I enter some kind of twilight zone in which sucking my boss's dick seems to make total sense."

He huffed in frustration. "God, I don't know how to put it into words. He's just—he's just a lot, you know? Larger than life. His presence just dominates everything and we all end up bending over backward to do everything he says."

"He sounds like a bully."

Nate smiled faintly. "I guess? It's hard to explain. He doesn't even need to say anything to make people scramble to please him."

Maya snorted. "Now that's a nice superpower to have." She shook her head. "I still think we should tell the police. Workplace sexual harassment should always be punished. *Any* sexual harassment should be punished."

Nate cringed. "Don't make me a victim. He's an enormous asshole, but I know he would have never forced me if I were smart enough to say no. He's too arrogant and proud to force anyone."

"Nate," Maya said, her voice unbearably gentle. "Victims of sexual harassment often deny that they were harassed."

Rubbing a hand over his face, Nate grimaced. "I know. But trust me, I know what I'm talking about. I know him, okay? He didn't even actually intend to use me that way. He's straight. All he wanted was to scare me off into quitting and make me lose the bet. But then we got pulled into this weird game of chicken, and the rest, as they say, is history."

She sighed. "Are you really all right, then? Really really all right?"

Nate shrugged, looking at his shoes. Shoes Ferrara had bought him.

Scowling, he toed them off. "I'm freaking out," he admitted.

"You just said you don't feel sexually harassed."

"I don't."

"Then why are you freaking out? Why now? You said you've been sucking his dick for weeks."

Nate felt his face become warm. He couldn't look his sister in the eye.

"Oh my god," Maya said.

Please don't say it.

"You actually like it!"

Nate glared at her. "I didn't like it—not at first. It was just a chore. But today I…" He trailed off, glaring at the cloudless sky outside the window.

"You what?"

Nate ran a hand over his face. Fuck, why was this so embarrassing to talk about? "I realized that it kind of turned me on—sucking him off."

The resulting silence was one of the most awkward in his life.

"Let me get it straight," Maya said slowly. "Sucking his dick was totally fine with you until you started liking it."

Nate pulled a face. "When you say it that way it makes me sound dumb."

"Because you're a dumbass," she said, throwing a pillow at his head.

Nate ducked. "It's just weird, okay? I'm straight. More importantly, I hate the guy!"

Maya let out a soft snort. "Is he hot?"

Scrunching up his nose, Nate shrugged. "How would I know? I'm straight."

His sister rolled her eyes. It was extremely annoying. "I'm straight, too, but I know a hot woman when I see one. Hot is hot."

"You can Google him," Nate grumbled. "Raffaele Ferrara."

She pulled out her phone.

"Damn," she said after a moment, looking at the screen.

Nate gave her an annoyed look. "He isn't that hot."

"He is. If it makes you feel better, sucking his dick would turn me on, too."

Now that was a mental image Nate really didn't need. Pursing his lips, he said nothing.

"So, what now?" Maya said when the silence lasted. "Are you quitting?"

Nate wanted to say yes.

He couldn't imagine being around Ferrara after what had happened. As dumb as it might make him sound, he'd never expected to get aroused from sucking his boss's dick—it could *never* happen again. But...

His ringtone prevented him from having to answer. Flinching, Nate pulled his phone out of his pocket.

Satan, the Caller ID said.

Nate's heart started beating faster.

"Is that him?"

Nate nodded miserably and answered the phone.

"Why are you not at work?" Ferrara said.

His voice was so cold it could have frozen hell.

Nate bit his bottom lip, suppressing the ridiculous urge to apologize. "It's almost six," he said in the most neutral tone he was capable of. "My workday is over."

"Your workday isn't over until I say so," Ferrara said tersely. "If I'm still at work, you are, too. You're my assistant."

"I don't think that word means what you think it means," Nate said. "It's not actually a synonym for 'slave.'"

"No, it isn't," the demon agreed. "Slaves don't get paid for overtime. Get to work. Now."

And he hung up.

Nate scowled at his phone before sighing and getting to his feet. "I have to go back to the office."

"Seriously? Tell him to fuck off and quit."

"Not yet. I can't lose the bet."

"Oh, for fuck's sake," Maya said, throwing up her hands in annoyance. "I can't believe you care that much about that stupid bet."

Nate glowered at her, deeply offended. "It isn't stupid at all. If I win, Ferrara will have to remove the microtransactions from my favorite franchise and give me a great recommendation letter. I've come this far, I can't quit ten days before I win the bet! I'm so close."

"And what if he tells you to suck his cock again? You'll say no?"

"Sure I will," Nate said.

The first thing Ferrara said when Nate entered his office was, "Come over here and finish it." His eyes were on his computer, but there was little doubt about what he meant.

Nate swallowed. "Seriously?" he said, stalling. "You told me to come back to the office because you wanted to get your cock wet?"

Ferrara still didn't deign to look at him. "I told you to come back because I didn't allow you to leave. Now get to work."

Nate should have told him to fuck off. He should have; he knew that.

But his legs were already moving.

Before he knew it, he was on his knees before his boss and he was pulling his half-hard cock out. "You have a functional right hand," he complained, licking the cockhead. *Mmm.* "You could have jerked off."

"Why would I jerk off when I have you?" Ferrara said, continuing to type as if Nate wasn't licking his hardening cock. His composure was infuriating.

"I'm your assistant, not your cocksucker," Nate grumbled before taking the cock into his mouth.

Don't get turned on, he begged his body.

Of course his body didn't listen. There was just something about the taste of Ferrara's cock, the scent of it, the way it felt stretching his lips to their limit, moving inside his sensitive mouth, against his tongue...

Fuck, it did turn him on. It was like being kissed with a cock. And he couldn't deny that the rush of power he felt from making *Ferrara* so hard for him only added to his arousal.

A moan slipped out of his mouth before he could stop it. Ferrara's thighs tensed under his hands.

Nate blushed. Even though his eyes were closed, he could feel Ferrara's gaze on him, heavy and evaluating.

"Are you actually enjoying this?" the bastard said, his voice mild and faintly amused. "I thought you were straight."

Nate opened his eyes and glared up at him. He pulled up with an obscene wet sound and said, "You have no room to talk. I'm not the one forcing my male assistant to suck my cock every day."

"Forcing?" Ferrara said, tilting his head, his eyes heavy-lidded. "You seem to be enjoying yourself."

Nate flushed. "You— You Stockholm-Syndrom'ed me into enjoying it!"

"I don't think it's a word."

"I hate you," Nate grumbled, and went back to sucking, just to avoid looking into those arrogant, knowing eyes. Asshole. He hated him. God, did he hate him.

"Do you?" Ferrara murmured, gripping his hair hard and then—

Nate moaned when he felt a hard leg between his thighs, pressing against his erection.

The bastard *chuckled*, thrusting into his mouth, using him, owning him. God, he hated him, hated him—

Nate came into his pants, grinding against his boss's leg and moaning weakly. Ferrara held him still, pumping his cock into his mouth and then spilling deep into his throat.

Nate swallowed greedily—and then promptly tried to look grossed out.

He finally let the softening cock out of his mouth and tucked it back into Ferrara's pants, his face very warm.

He got to his feet, trying to act like his pants didn't have a wet spot.

If the asshole mocked him for that, he was going to fucking punch him.

"I think we should talk about finding a replacement for me," Nate said, clearing his throat.

Ferrara looked up from fixing his belt. "What."

Crossing his arms over his chest, Nate said, "My replacement. You do remember that the six months will be over in ten days, right?" He smiled. "I hope you have already talked to the game monetization director about removing the MTX from Rangers 5."

Ferrara stared at him with an unreadable look. "You're still going on about your ridiculous bet."

Ridiculous bet?

Incredulous, Nate laughed. "Of course I am. That's why I'm still here. And don't be such a sore loser. The bet isn't ridiculous just because you lost. Don't you dare backtrack now. You promised."

Ferrara's gaze moved back to his computer. "Fine," he said, but it still wasn't very reassuring. Nate didn't like the strange, calculating look in his eyes at all.

"I'll tell HR to start looking for a new PA," Nate said when the silence stretched.

"It's not necessary," Ferrara said, starting to type something. "My staff is very thorough. I'm sure that's already taken care of."

"Right," Nate said. "You also promised a recommendation letter."

Ferrara's lips twisted. "Don't worry, I keep my word," he said. "You may go now."

Nate was frowning as he turned to leave. Although Ferrara had seemingly agreed to keep his end of the deal, something about the exchange made him feel uneasy and unsettled.

He just didn't believe it was going to be that easy.

Chapter 9

The HR department did have a replacement lined up, apparently.

Connor McDonough was an extremely capable PA with years of experience working for executives of big companies.

Frankly, he made Nate feel awkward and self-conscious about his own, very limited job experience. It was kind of difficult to teach your replacement when that replacement was far more capable at this job than you were.

"Don't worry, I've got it," Connor said, smiling his perfect little smile as he gently took the notebook from Nate and followed Ferrara into the conference room.

Nate was left standing there, looking at the door that closed in his face.

Okay.

It was fine.

It wasn't like he even liked this job or something. Connor-the-perfect-PA could totally keep acting like he could do everything better than Nate. He probably really could. It shouldn't have bothered him.

And it didn't. Not at all. Nate was fucking ecstatic. It was nice to just chill for a while at his desk, doing nothing productive.

Nate was playing solitaire when Ferrara and Connor finally returned from the meeting.

He probably shouldn't have taken such pleasure from seeing the hurried, nervous look on Connor's face as he timidly followed their boss. The boss in question exuded irritation in tangible waves, his jaw clenched and his face like stone. For once, Satan's insufferable attitude was very welcome. It made Nate feel less useless when Ferrara fixed him with a heavy look out of black eyes and motioned to his office with his head.

Violently quashing the urge to follow the silent order, Nate didn't move. He smiled. "I'm sure your new assistant can assist you, sir."

A muscle twitched in Ferrara's temple. For a moment, he said nothing, just looking at Nate.

Then, that familiar glint appeared in his eyes. "Come to think of it, you're right. Connor."

Before Nate could process that, Connor followed Ferrara into his office. The door closed with a thud.

Nate stared at it, feeling… he didn't know what. Had the asshole really meant that he was going to use Connor that way?

But then again, why wouldn't he? It was apparently part of the job description now. What difference did it make for Ferrara? A mouth was a mouth. It wasn't like Ferrara was attracted to Nate—or other men, for that matter. It was just stress relief for him, nothing more.

It was still utterly disgusting. Forcing a guy who hadn't even started working for him officially to suck his cock… it was… it was reprehensible. *Despicable*. Now poor Connor would feel obligated to do it to get the job. Nate obviously couldn't allow that to happen. It was sexual harassment!

He got to his feet and strode to the door. He pushed it, but it didn't budge.

It was locked.

Nate stared at it, indignation making him see red. Satan had never bothered to lock the door for Nate's sake, but apparently Connor-the-perfect-PA deserved that consideration.

Clenching his jaw, Nate knocked sharply.

For a long, excruciating moment no one answered. But then again, who would answer? Connor was probably too busy sucking Ferrara's thick cock, slurping all over it like a whore—

The door opened.

"Yes?" Connor said.

Nate narrowed his eyes, studying him suspiciously. He didn't seem out of breath. And his lips didn't look red and well-used like Nate's own lips often did after sucking Ferrara's cock.

"Why was the door locked?" he said testily.

Connor blinked. "I locked it for Mr. Ferrara's privacy while he changed. That's what any good PA would do."

Nate curled his fingers into a fist. "Right," he said, looking over Connor's shoulder.

Ferrara's dark eyes met his. He really was changing, his white shirt half-unbuttoned, revealing his muscular chest and stomach.

Nate pursed his lips and turned away.

He was fuming as he returned to his desk, feeling annoyed and angry for no damn reason.

Fuck, he couldn't wait for everything to be over.

He hated this, hated Ferrara and his arrogant face and his stupid cock and his insufferable attitude.

He couldn't wait to be rid of him.

***

If there was one good thing about Connor's presence, it was that he was *always* there. He followed Nate everywhere when he wasn't tripping over his feet to be helpful and show that he was the better PA. That meant that there literally was no opportunity for Nate to perform… his unofficial responsibilities.

Speaking plainly, he hadn't sucked or touched his boss's cock in nine days. Not that he was counting or anything.

It was just… weird.

Nate sometimes entertained the thought that Ferrara's increasingly foul mood over the week might have had something to do with not having his cock sucked any time he wanted, but it was unlikely that he didn't get laid by someone else. Nate wouldn't know: Connor was now the one in possession of Ferrara's work phone and he might have been arranging the boss's booty calls every day for all Nate knew.

Nate didn't ask. Something always kept him from asking.

Before Nate knew it, it was his last day at the Caldwell Group and he was saying his goodbyes to his co-workers. Former co-workers now.

"I wish you'd stay," Brenda said, hugging him. "You can manage him so much better than the other assistants he's had."

"Me, managing him?" Nate said with a laugh. "Is that a joke?"

Brenda shook her head with a rueful smile. "You weren't here. You can't see the difference between how he was with them and you."

The subject was starting to make him uncomfortable, so Nate changed it and went to say his goodbyes to the guys in other departments. Saying goodbye felt a little bittersweet. He may not have wanted this job, but it was the first real job he'd ever had and he'd made a lot of friends.

By the time he finished, it was evening and there was only one thing left.

He returned to the top floor.

Connor was seated at Nate's—his own desk.

Ignoring the weirdly uncomfortable feeling in his stomach, Nate smiled. "I'm leaving. He's in, right?"

Connor nodded, glancing at the closed door. "He doesn't seem to be in a good mood," he said timidly. All the confidence and smugness he had exuded last week was now gone. Now he seemed as scared of Ferrara as Brenda was.

It shouldn't have pleased Nate.

"Nothing I haven't seen before," he said with a shrug and entered the office without knocking.

He closed the door and stared at the man seated behind the desk.

Raffaele Ferrara. Satan in a Dolce & Gabbana suit. The horrible boss who had worked Nate like a personal slave for the past half a year.

He was free of him now.

Free.

The thought was... strange. It didn't seem real. He didn't feel the satisfaction, the closure he had expected to feel.

When Ferrara lifted his gaze from his computer, they just looked at each other in silence.

Nate moistened his lips with his tongue. "I'm leaving."

The other man said nothing, his expression unreadable.

Swallowing, Nate crossed his arms over his chest. "Do you have the recommendation letter?"

Ferrara nodded, glancing at the piece of paper on his desk.

Nate walked over and picked it up. He read it with some suspicion, but it was a perfectly good recommendation letter. A great one, even.

Lifting his gaze, Nate peered at Ferrara suspiciously. "What about removing the microtransactions from Rangers 5?"

Ferrara shrugged. "I ordered the monetization department to tone them down and make the MTX mostly cosmetic. Removing them completely isn't feasible—the game was designed around them."

"But you promised," Nate said. "You shouldn't have bet on something you can't do."

"I didn't *promise* it. I humored you." A strange expression passed over Ferrara's face. "Frankly, I expected you to quit within a few weeks. I didn't know how annoyingly stubborn you were."

Nate scoffed, but it wasn't hard to believe, knowing Ferrara's arrogance. He always thought he was right.

"Fine," he said sullenly. "As long as they remove the invasive pay-to-win stuff, I can live with cosmetic microtransactions."

Ferrara said nothing, just gazing at him with the same unreadable look.

Nate wet his lips again. "I guess this is it, then?"

He didn't know what he expected, but it was oddly disappointing when Ferrara just nodded and turned back to his computer.

Right.

All right.

This was fine.

"Bye," Nate said bitingly, feeling annoyed and maybe even a little upset at being dismissed as if he were nothing. Unimportant. Replaceable. Just a minor bug under Raffaele Ferrara's expensive shoe. He probably wouldn't even remember Nate's name in a month. He didn't know why that thought bothered him so much.

The bastard said nothing, still looking at his computer.

Nate slammed the door shut on his way out.

Chapter 10

"Nothing yet?" Maya said when she came home.

Nate shook his head, avoiding her pitying eyes. He didn't look away from the video game he was playing, but it was hard to keep the confident façade when it had been his fourth job interview that didn't result in anything but vague promises to call him back. Spoiler alert: they didn't call him back.

"I don't get it," Maya said, plopping down on his bed. "I was so sure you'd got this. That job sounded perfect for you."

Nate shrugged. "I guess there were better candidates," he said.

His sister made a sound of disagreement.

Feeling a rush of fondness for her, Nate forced a smile for Maya's sake. "It's fine, really," he said. "I'm not in a hurry to get another job. I have a pretty nice financial cushion after…"

"Sucking your ex-boss's cock?" Maya said with a smirk.

Nate glowered at her but didn't say anything. He knew Maya just wanted to rile him up and take his mind off any depressing thoughts.

Propping herself on an elbow, Maya glanced at the computer screen. "Don't tell me you've been playing this game all day again."

"Not all day," Nate said, somewhat defensively. "I just need to make sure he really keeps his end of the deal and doesn't put the microtransactions back."

Maya rolled her eyes. "And what are you going to do if he does? It's not like you signed a legally binding contract. Let it go. Forget about him. Move on."

"You're the one who keeps reminding me of him," Nate grumbled, even though his heart wasn't in it.

Lately his heart wasn't really in anything.

He had to admit that ever since he'd quit his job, it was hard to summon much enthusiasm for anything. He must have gotten so used to the hectic, insane pace of his life as Raffaele Ferrara's PA, that his normal life seemed... boring now. *Dull*.

It didn't help that all his job applications had been rejected, and he had nothing to keep his mind busy with. So it totally wasn't Nate's fault that he still kept thinking about his ex-boss—sometimes. He thought about him only *sometimes*: only when he saw his expensive suits in his closet or wore the shoes Ferrara had paid for. Well, he also thought of him every time he saw his own dick and cataloged differences between his and Ferrara's (his cock was just a little shorter, but nowhere near as thick as Ferrara's).

The most embarrassing, weirdest part was, the sight of his own cock turned him on now. Like, who got turned on at the sight of his own cock? He was a weirdo, apparently.

And then it got worse.

That night, Nate was watching porn in his bedroom, the door shut and locked to prevent his sister from walking in.

He needed some quality time with his right hand, so he stripped down and stretched on his back.

He looked at the porn. A curvy redhead was touching herself sensually, running her hands over her amazing tits.

It looked so hot. But somehow, Nate's gaze kept drifting to the male porn star's cock. He was well endowed, his cock thick and big, kind of similar to...

Nate's mouth filled with saliva.

Fuck, he couldn't look away from that cock. He nearly whined when the redhead licked the head before taking the cock into her mouth.

Nate shoved two fingers into his mouth. He moaned around them, his other hand stroking his erection frantically. But it wasn't enough. He wanted a cock in his mouth. He wanted a fat cock stretching his lips.

Nate looked down at his cock, his eyes glassy with arousal. He wanted... Fuck, he wanted to taste it. Hell, he'd always been very flexible. It was worth a try.

He shoved a pillow under his back and lifted his legs to his head. For a moment, he thought it wouldn't work, but then his cock was right there, long and hard. Nate leaned forward and licked the head, whining at the double sensation. Fuck, it felt so good. He took the cockhead into his mouth and sucked, swirling his tongue around it, ignoring the pain in his neck and back.

"Suck it, suck that cock, yeah," the porn star said. "You're such a cock slut, aren't you?"

The over-the-top lines that normally made Nate roll his eyes just turned him on now. He squeezed his eyes shut, sucking on the head and wishing he could take the cock deeper, wishing there were hands gripping his hair and holding him still as Ferrara thrust into his mouth, infuriatingly arrogant and bossy—

He came, moaning around his own cock weakly.

He swallowed his jizz and let his legs fall.

Still panting, Nate stared at the ceiling dazedly.

Fuck.

***

All right, apparently fantasizing about sucking a cock—and even wanting to suck a cock—was fairly normal for straight guys. At least that was what Google and Reddit told Nate. That was a little reassuring. Not that he would necessarily freak out if he turned out to be bi—his parents were awesome and Nate was pretty sure Maya was into some weird gay werewolf porn—but Nate just genuinely didn't think he was attracted to men. The idea of having sex with men, kissing them and getting naked with them was just... *odd*. He didn't think he was attracted to men. It was just the idea of sucking a hard, thick cock that got him all hot and bothered. And if the cock in his fantasies was shaped like his horrible ex-boss's, it was probably totally normal, considering that it was the only cock he'd ever sucked—besides his own.

So, what did that mean? Apparently he was just a straight weirdo brainwashed into wanting to suck cock.

Maya laughed at him when he told her that.

"I think you just need to get out and get laid," she said, grinning. "By a woman with a cock, if that's what you're into."

Nate frowned. "I don't like one-night stands. You know that."

The look Maya gave him was something between fond and exasperated. "Then don't make it a one-night stand. You don't have a job yet—why don't you use that free time to get a nice girlfriend—or a nice *someone*."

"I'm not into guys," Nate said with a chuckle, shaking his head. "I'm serious about it, Maya. I'm not in denial. I can't imagine wanting to kiss another man."

His sister's expression was full of skepticism. "You won't know until you try it. Seriously, get out and get laid. You're starting to depress me too with your constant moping."

"I'm not moping."

"Oh, really? Please. If I didn't know better, I'd think you were fired from your job instead of quitting. You're totally moping, dumbass."

That was the thing about living with a sibling: they knew you too well to buy your bullshit.

Nate sighed and leaned back in his chair, running a hand over his face. "All right, yeah," he admitted quietly, looking at the logo of RD Software under Rangers 5's. "I feel so down, and fuck, I'm not even sure *why*. I should be happy, right? I won the bet, I proved him wrong. But I feel…" He shrugged, unable to articulate it.

Maya smiled crookedly, raking her fingers through Nate's hair. "Ever thought you might have actually liked your job?"

Nate laughed, but it sounded shaky and unconvincing even to him. "Don't be ridiculous," he said faintly. "I've never wanted to be a PA. I'll find a new job soon—a better job—and I'll get over this. I'm sure of it."

Except finding a new job turned out to be much harder than Nate had expected.

Over the next few weeks, he applied for job after job, without any success. On the rare occasion that he was called for an interview, they seemed to like him well enough during the interviews, but he hadn't heard back from any of them.

Nate couldn't deny that it was very disheartening, and his mood hadn't been exactly improving as weeks went by.

His phone rang four weeks after he'd left the Caldwell Group.

"Hello?" Nate said groggily, yawning and trying to blink himself awake.

"Hi Nate. It's Olivia Mendez, the Caldwell Group's HR assistant. How are you?"

Nate sat up, all sleep gone in an instant. He thought he said something, but he wasn't even sure, his heart beating fast and his pulse thundering in his ears. He suddenly felt alive and wide awake. The Caldwell Group. What did *he* want?

He must have asked that, because Olivia didn't waste time on small talk. "I wanted to let you know that the position of Mr. Ferrara's PA is open again, in case you were interested." Her voice was full of skepticism—she clearly didn't believe that anyone would be eager to return to that job—and yet she was still calling him.

"Did he tell you to call me?" Nate said. "Ferrara?"

"Well, yes," Olivia said. "His new PA, Abel, quit yesterday—"

"I thought his name was Connor."

"Connor was fired two weeks ago," Olivia said, a grimace in her voice.

Nate didn't feel bad for him. Did that make him a terrible person? It probably made him a terrible person.

Maybe his ex-boss's horribleness had rubbed off on him.

"So Mr. Ferrara told me to call you and get you back," Olivia said, her tone a little apologetic. "I told him that you'd likely found another job already, but he seemed so confident that you haven't. I'm sorry for bothering you. I'll tell him no, obviously."

Nate stared blankly in front of him.

I told him that you'd likely found another job already, but he seemed so confident that you haven't.

"That son-of-a-bitch," he hissed, his disbelief mixed with rising anger.

"Excuse me?" Olivia said.

"Sorry, just thinking aloud," Nate said, his mind racing. Now all of these rejected job applications made a horrible amount of sense.

At the same time, they made no sense whatsoever. Why would Ferrara even bother ruining Nate's job prospects? Raffaele Ferrara was a very important man. He was the COO and vice president of the Caldwell Group, a man with a ridiculously busy schedule—Nate knew that better than anyone. Nate couldn't understand why the fuck the asshole had bothered to make sure Nate couldn't get another job. Was it spite? Just because Nate had won their little bet? Ferrara was a dick, but Nate hadn't thought he was that petty.

"What do you want me to tell him?" Olivia said.

"Tell him to fuck off," Nate said.

"I... I can't tell him that, but I'll tell him that you said no."

Nate glowered at the wall. No, that wasn't satisfying at all. "You know what? I think I'll drop by and tell him what I think of him in person."

Also, Nate fucking deserved an explanation, and then Satan deserved a fist to his face. Nate wasn't particularly picky about the order.

Chapter 11

The reception room outside Satan's office looked exactly the same: intimidatingly fancy and intimidatingly quiet, as if people were afraid to breathe wrong.

Brenda smiled in obvious relief when she saw him.

"I'm so glad you are back!" she said, half-whispering for some reason, as if Satan had super-hearing and could hear them through the closed door. "Olivia was so sure you wouldn't return, but I hoped she was wrong."

"Why?" Nate said, dropping a kiss on her cheek and studying her. "How are you? You look tired."

Brenda sighed, glancing at the closed door warily. "I am tired. He's been in a mood lately."

"Isn't he always?" Nate said with a snort.

Wincing, Brenda shook her head. "He's been worse. Or we just got used to him being nicer."

Nate looked at her incredulously.

Brenda chuckled, tucking a stray lock of her hair behind her ear. "I know you don't believe me, but he really was nicer when you were around. Less harsh."

"Right, he just took out his bad temper on me," Nate said, rolling his eyes with a smile.

She raised her eyebrows. "Well, he certainly took out his temper on Connor and Abel, but it didn't seem to help. Abel left in tears yesterday, literally. I've never seen a grown man cry."

Nate scrunched up his nose, unconvinced. He still didn't buy that Ferrara could somehow be *more* horrible than he had been with him.

"It doesn't matter," he said. "I'm not here to stay."

Her face fell.

Nate refused to feel guilty about it. "I just want to talk to him for a moment."

She frowned, glancing uncertainly at the door. "He's busy. He has a meeting with the marketing head right now."

"You know what? I don't care," Nate said. "That's the perk of not being his employee-slash-personal slave anymore. I don't have to shake in my boots every time His Highness frowns. He's not the boss of me."

He strode confidently toward the door, ignoring Brenda's feeble protests.

Except his confidence seemed to evaporate the moment he opened the door and was pinned under the heavy gaze of those black eyes.

Nate swallowed. He tried to summon the anger he'd felt just a few moments ago, but his thoughts kept scattering, the familiar urge to please this man creeping back. It was utterly disgusting.

Someone coughed a little, and Nate wrenched his eyes away from Ferrara's.

He stared at the portly man, feeling his confidence and purpose come back now that he wasn't looking at *him* anymore. "Hello, Mr. Jameson. How are you? Would you mind stepping out of the room while I talk to him?"

Jameson glanced helplessly at Ferrara.

Satan said nothing, looking at Nate with a strange expression. There was a hint of irritation there, definitely, but other than that, it was hard to tell.

"Leave," he said at last, still looking at Nate.

Nate didn't move, knowing the order wasn't for him. It was kind of revolting how well he could still read this man and know the difference between Ferrara being a jerk toward him and toward someone else.

It seemed Jameson wasn't as well versed in the demonic language as Nate was. He looked between Nate and Ferrara, his uncertainty obvious.

Nate took pity on him. "He's addressing you," he clarified.

When Ferrara didn't deny that, Jameson hurried toward the door so fast it surprised Nate. The guy must have been in better shape than he looked.

The door shut behind Jameson with a soft click, and silence fell upon the room.

Since he didn't have any excuse not to look at him anymore, Nate met Ferrara's eyes again and tried to give him his angriest look.

He *was* angry, dammit.

He was here to tell Ferrara exactly what he thought of him.

But all that came out of his mouth was, "Why?"

When Ferrara just tilted his head slightly, Nate glared at him. "Why did you do that?"

The asshole quirked a black eyebrow. "I have no idea what you're talking about."

Nate clenched his fists. "You made them all reject me," he ground out. "All my job applications. All twelve of them. Don't tell me you had nothing to do with it."

The second eyebrow joined the first. A sardonic smile touched Ferrara's lips. It didn't touch his eyes. He truly looked like a demon. A creepy demon with eyes as black as hell.

"I'm flattered you think I'm omnipotent, but I'm not," Ferrara said mildly, his soft voice completely at odds with the hard, intense look in his eyes. "People search for jobs for months and months. Maybe you simply weren't qualified for the jobs you have applied for."

Nate's nails dug into his palms. "I was qualified for those jobs. I was overqualified for some of them. But apparently, despite the glowing recommendation letter you gave me, I'm not even good enough for the job of a QA tester. Amazing, isn't it?"

"It does seem a little strange," Ferrara said.

Was that amusement in his voice? It figured that the dick would derive amusement from someone's misery.

Nate glowered at him. "How did you do it?"

Ferrara gave a shrug.

"*Why* did you do it?" Nate said. "I didn't think you were that spiteful. I thought even you wouldn't stoop so low."

"I was simply making a point."

Nate laughed. "And what point is that? Please enlighten me."

"I didn't say you could go. Until I say so, no one is allowed to leave this company."

Nate stared at him. "You need help. Like, professional help." He chuckled, shaking his dead. "Newsflash, asshole: we live in a free country. Your employees aren't your slaves. Maybe things are different in Italy in some bumfuck Sicilian town or something, but you're not there. The US Constitution. Give it a read sometime. Spoiler alert: no man has absolute power, not even the President."

Ferrara didn't look fazed in the slightest. "You're to return to work effective immediately. Go to HR and sign the contract. It's ready."

Nate didn't know whether to laugh or punch him in the face. It was like talking to a wall. "How are you even real? You're like the stereotypical horrible boss on steroids on top of an insufferable egomaniac who can't take no for an answer! No, I'm not going to be your goddamn PA—I'm a game designer, not a glorified manservant! I want to make games instead of running errands for you—or for anyone else. Is that so hard to grasp?"

For a moment, Nate thought Satan wasn't even going to bother replying to him.

But at last, Ferrara spoke.

"You want to work on making games." It was a statement.

"Yes!" Nate huffed. "Did you honestly think being a PA was my life's ambition? I've always been clear about why I became your PA. I thought we were on the same page about it." He paused, as something occurred to him just then. Raffaele Ferrara wanted him back as his PA. It was probably stupid that he hadn't thought about the implications of it before.

Ferrara wanted him back.

He wanted Nate back badly enough to go the extra mile and stop other companies from hiring him.

Nate cocked his head to the side, eyeing his ex-boss thoughtfully as he tried to digest that. "You said you did it because no one is allowed to leave the company until you say so. That's bullshit. I'm sure plenty of people have quit in the past. Heck, your latest PA quit yesterday—because apparently you reduced him to tears. But here you are, bullying *me* into coming back. What gives? What, Connor and Abel refused to suck your cock or something? Or did you like my mouth better?"

Although it was just snark, he saw Ferrara's gaze flick down to his mouth. It was blink-and-you'd-miss-it fast, but since Nate was still unhealthily attuned to the infinitesimal changes in Ferrara's expression, he didn't miss the look.

He laughed, equally incredulous, furious—and absurdly pleased. God, this was fucked-up. Why the hell did he feel *pleased*?

"Seriously?" Nate said. "Wow, I'm flattered."

The look Ferrara gave him could have frozen hell. "If you really think your mediocre blowjob skills are the reason I want you back, you're delusional. You're simply less incompetent than my other assistants, and training another semi-competent PA is a waste of my time."

Nate smiled sweetly at him. "Right. Then I guess you wouldn't mind not having my mediocre blowjob skills at your disposal anymore. Even if I were to come back, I wouldn't suck your dick again."

"So you are coming back."

Nate thought about it for a moment. He did like this company and its people—present company excluded. He could come back, but on his terms.

"I have conditions," Nate said. "First, I'll be your PA only until the end of the year." He raised his hand, forestalling any objections. "In the meantime I'll find and train up a good PA for you, someone who won't have a nervous breakdown every time you frown. After that, you'll transfer me to the game design department and leave me alone."

Those black eyes stared at him for a few seconds before their owner nodded.

Feeling a little suspicious of how easily Ferrara had agreed to his conditions, Nate continued.

"And I'm not sucking your dick again. I'm serious about it. If I'm to really stay and work for this company, I don't want my coworkers to think I got my job by sucking the boss's cock."

Ferrara's expression flickered for a moment, becoming less impassive, but then it was smoothed back into the inscrutable mask he normally wore. "Fine," he said.

"And I want a raise," Nate said, knowing that he was pushing his luck, but curious how far Ferrara was willing to go to have him back. "I want my salary doubled." That was a ridiculous demand—he'd already been paid very well.

But Ferrara just gave a clipped nod.

Nate looked at him incredulously, but okay, he wasn't going to look a gift horse in the mouth.

"All right, then," he said. "I'll go to HR now."

Ferrara just turned back to his computer, and taking it for the dismissal it was, Nate left, his mind still reeling.

God, did this man have some kind of superpower of bending other people's wills? Nate had come here to tell the asshole what he thought of him, but instead he had somehow ended up accepting his job offer. It made no damn sense.

His sister wasn't going to be impressed.

***

It was disturbingly easy to slip back into the role of Raffaele Ferrara's PA.

Nate was kind of embarrassed to admit it, but he'd really missed the challenge of it and the absolutely crazy, hectic pace of his life.

What he *didn't* miss was the way his world once again revolved around his horrible boss. Nate felt like he spent every waking moment either with Ferrara, or thinking about him and his orders and needs.

Speaking of Ferrara's *needs*, there was one need that remained not addressed. And it was becoming increasingly difficult to ignore. Nate could feel the tension and frustration mounting in Ferrara with every passing day, betrayed by the sharpness of his voice and the shortness of his temper.

It was also betrayed by the way those black eyes sometimes tracked his lips when Nate spoke. It made Nate warm and fidgety, his mouth going dry as he imagined—

He adamantly quashed those traitorous thoughts, but they kept resurfacing. Fuck, he really needed to find a nice woman who'd let him suck her cock, so that he'd stop imagining sucking his boss's. But now that his life revolved around Ferrara again, he had no time for anything resembling a personal life.

So he just pushed those thoughts down and tried to ignore the way Ferrara's eyes flicked to his mouth when Nate licked his lips. Or the way Ferrara's suit pants stretched obscenely over the bulge in his crotch. Or the way his own cock stirred as he imagined dropping down in front of his boss, yanking his zipper down and swallowing that big, thick—

Ugh.

All right, the "not thinking about it" part was still a work in progress.

Chapter 12

Raffaele Ferrara sat at the head of the conference table, his face impassive and cold, betraying nothing of the frustration brimming under his skin.

Few could probably guess that he wasn't paying any attention to the meeting, but it was small comfort.

"…as you see, Mr. Ferrara, everything is in order. The deal will be beneficial to both of our companies…"

The manager of Typhoon Enterprises was still saying something, but Raffaele could barely hear what the man was saying, the low hum of arousal and frustration buzzing beneath his skin making it difficult to focus.

Fuck, this was… *unacceptable*. How had he allowed the situation to come to this?

It should have never come to this.

He'd always been so careful. For a reason.

One of Raffaele's earliest memories was that of his grandmother. Nonna Francesca had been a bold, strong woman with sharp black eyes on her handsome, aging face. He remembered her smiling wryly as she joked about how men in the Ferrara family were blessed with "high drive." Then she and Aunt Barbara would exchange a knowing look and laugh about it, as if sharing an inside joke. Raffaele's mother had never cracked a smile if she was present.

It would be years before he was old enough to understand why.

Men in the Ferrara family really were blessed with a high sex drive. Or more like, cursed with it.

Raffaele's father, Marco, unashamedly loved sex, and his wife didn't satisfy his sexual appetites. Last time Raffaele saw his father, Marco had had two women in his bed—women who weren't his wife. It was no surprise, of course. It was one of the reasons he had moved to America—he couldn't stay in Italy anymore without punching his father and snapping at his mother to grow a spine and finally leave the man who didn't respect her in the least. Obviously there were other reasons. More important reasons. But Marco's shameless infidelity and the depressing atmosphere at home had definitely contributed to his decision.

The aggravating part was, Raffaele felt like a hypocrite for judging his father. He had never gone without frequent, regular sex since his early teenage years. But when he'd left Italy, he had been just eighteen. He'd thought his high libido was a natural thing for a young man in his late teens, that he couldn't possibly have his father's… affliction.

As a grown man of thirty-two, Raffaele could only shake his head at his eighteen-year-old self's naïveté.

His libido hadn't diminished with age. If anything, it had grown. He couldn't properly focus on work if he hadn't gotten laid in a few days. It lessened his efficiency. Distracted him. In that way, he was very much his father's son.

Raffaele honestly wasn't sure if the men in his family had some kind of hypersexuality disorder or if they just had a very high sex drive. The three doctors that he'd consulted had completely different opinions. One of them saw no issue with his sex drive and confirmed that there were some studies that proved that a high sex drive really was inherited. The second doctor had seen "some cause for concern" and suggested drugs to reduce his libido. The third had tried to *psychoanalyze* him—it went without saying that Raffaele had walked out.

In any case, regardless of whether it was normal or not, the end result was the same. That was why Raffaele didn't do relationships: he didn't want to reduce any woman to the depressed mess his mother had become. After his last attempt at a relationship a decade ago, he had no delusions. He didn't trust himself to be a better partner than Marco was.

But unlike his father, Raffaele didn't like one-night stands or prostitutes. He didn't like having sex with women he didn't know. Although he always used condoms, he still liked the certainty that he wasn't in danger of catching STDs. Which presented something of a problem, given his avoidance of relationships and refusal to pay for sex.

The "booty calls," as his insolent PA called them, were a necessity: they were women he'd known for a while who wanted the same thing he did—frequent sex with a skilled partner and nothing more. It was honest and mutually beneficial. It was a good way to deal with his libido without it ever becoming a serious problem. It was a good solution. Or rather, it had been.

He didn't want to call one of those women now.

He wanted his assistant—his very male assistant—to get on his knees and suck his cock.

The cock in question twitched in his pants, and Raffaele gritted his teeth, beyond aggravated.

It was his own damn fault. He should have never bullied Nate into returning to work for him. He should have left him alone.

But he was a creature of habit. He'd grown... *used* to Nate and his insolent remarks and the way the boy could almost read his thoughts and wishes before Raffaele even said them aloud. He had wanted him back, because the sight of Connor and Abel at Nate's desk had only irritated him. So he had wanted Nate back and he had gotten him back, because he always got what he wanted. In that way he was also his father's son.

The thought made Raffaele's lips curl into a self-deprecating smile. Unfortunately, being aware of his faults did nothing to eliminate them.

He had gotten Nate back. He was back—but things still weren't back to normal. His body seemed to think that "normal" should include having his assistant's mouth around his cock every day.

Christ, it was ridiculous. He was straight. He'd never been attracted to men, no matter how sexually frustrated he was.

The whole thing with Nate had started because he was bored and it had been entertaining to watch the boy glare at him and swallow his cutting remarks in order not to get fired and win his ridiculous bet. It had amused him. Raffaele had just wanted to anger Nate enough to make him snap and give up. He hadn't actually thought that Nate would follow his orders and get him off—with his hand and then later with his mouth.

Raffaele had always tried to be honest with himself. He wasn't a very good man. He would be the first to admit that his moral compass was somewhat skewed, and he tended to treat people like things if he wasn't careful. It had been often remarked that he lacked qualities like compassion and human decency. But he'd always drawn the line at having sex with his employees.

It wasn't something he ever did. Frankly, he simply found it unappealing. What was the challenge in fucking women who were too scared to say no? He could never be certain that they actually wanted him.

Nate was different. He wasn't scared of him.

Or rather, of course he had been scared of him—at first. But by the time the whole arrangement between them had started, Nate had become too comfortable with him to truly be scared. He talked back. He used "sir" only when he felt like it. He grumbled and bitched if he found a task unpleasant until Raffaele caved and assigned it to someone else. Raffaele had been too soft with him even before Nate started sucking his cock.

His cock twitched again. Raffaele hissed in annoyance, shifting lower in his seat.

He glanced around the conference room, but of course no one had seen it, because everyone avoided looking his way.

Everyone but Nate.

He was seated at the small desk to the side of the conference table. But he wasn't taking notes. He was frowning, looking at Raffaele.

Raffaele glared at him, his irritation spiking when his gaze dropped to Nate's soft, full lips, slightly parted. It would be so easy to walk over, unzip his pants, and slide his cock into that mouth, and damn everyone watching—

"If you find our conditions satisfactory, please sign here, Mr. Ferrara."

Raffaele shifted his gaze to the contract in front of him and skimmed it with his eyes, without even seeing it. He couldn't fucking focus, his cock throbbing in his pants.

Someone handed him a pen.

"Please sign here."

Raffaele put the pen against the paper, ready to sign and get it over with, when Nate cleared his throat. Loudly. "Can I talk to you, sir?"

He turned his head to him. Everyone in the room did. It *was* a massive breach of protocol. Personal assistants weren't supposed to interrupt important negotiations like these.

Nate gave him a look that was between pleading and stubborn.

"Now?" Raffaele said.

"Yes, sir. It won't take more than a few minutes."

Irritated but curious, Raffaele got to his feet and strode into the smaller room that adjoined the main conference room. It was a good thing his suit jacket was long enough to cover his crotch.

Nate closed the door behind them and hissed, "What the hell were you doing? You were about to sign a contract with so many loopholes even I could see it!"

Raffaele opened his mouth and then closed it, not knowing what to say.

If Nate was right, he had no excuse for his inattention.

Nate huffed, glancing down at Raffaele's crotch. He flushed, scowled, and looked back at Raffaele's face. "Is it really that bad? I didn't know your brain relocated to your dick when you were horny."

"Watch your tone."

Nate raised his eyebrows. "Or what? You'll fire me?" He glanced at the door, chewing on his lip. "When was the last time you got laid?"

"None of your business," Raffaele bit out, trying not to imagine shoving his insolent PA to his knees and then shoving his cock down his throat.

"That long, huh?" Nate said, before heaving a long-suffering sigh. He dropped to his knees. "I'm doing this for the company," he said, unzipping Raffaele's fly.

Raffaele couldn't care less about his reasons, his fingers burying in Nate's hair and pulling his face to his cock.

"Impatient," his infuriating PA said and then *finally* fit his warm, wet mouth around his aching cock.

Raffaele bit the inside of his cheek to keep himself from making any sound. His hips were moving without his volition, his cock pistoning in and out of the boy's mouth as his hand gripped his hair. He stared greedily at Nate's flushed face, at his plump lips stretched wide around his cock, those glazed eyes wide and disbelieving, as if Nate couldn't believe what he was doing.

Nate lifted his gaze and they *looked* at each other as Raffaele fucked his mouth. Somehow, it made the act ten times more obscene, making him painfully aware that he was fucking his male assistant's mouth while his business partners were just a thin wall away. He could *hear* them talk, fuck. He wondered if they could hear the wet, slurpy sounds Nate's mouth made, too. Even if they could, he didn't care. He needed to fuck this mouth, this insolent, disrespectful, infuriating mouth that never shut up. He needed to fuck Nate's throat raw, so that his voice became so wrecked he couldn't talk back at him for days.

It took him a humiliatingly short time to come, but he was so worked up it wasn't surprising. He groaned lowly, keeping Nate's head still as he fucked his throat the last few times, grinding his cockhead against it as he spilled his jizz down his throat.

Nate moaned, his gaze unfocused. The little shit totally got off on this.

"Thanks," Raffaele said dryly, tucking his cock back into his pants and fixing his clothes. "Your sacrifice for the company's good has been noted."

Nate glared at him. "Fuck you," he croaked out, his lips still red and puffy and *used*—

Raffaele averted his eyes and strode toward the door, annoyed with himself.

***

Nate was still scowling as the door shut behind Ferrara.

Asshole.

Fuck, how he *hated* him.

Nate jerked his fly open and stroked his aching cock, hard and fast, pushing the fingers of his other hand into his mouth. He moaned around them and jacked his cock. He could still taste Ferrara's come in his mouth, so it didn't take long.

He spilled into his hand, hating Ferrara and hating himself.

God, he was fucking messed-up in the head.

He had *promised*. He had promised to himself that he wouldn't fall into the same rabbit hole, that he'd stay away from his horrible boss's cock, but the moment he was given the flimsiest excuse to suck it, he'd done just that.

Unbelievable. Pathetic.

Shaking his head, Nate cleaned his hand, fixed his clothes as best as he could, and returned to the conference room.

Satan was seated in his chair, his body language once again relaxed, his gaze hard and razor-sharp as he bored a hole in the Typhoon Enterprises' executive, who was stammering excuses as he tried—and failed—to convince Ferrara the contract they were offering was good.

Ferrara didn't even glance at him as Nate took his seat, which only annoyed Nate further, though rationally he was glad of it. The fact that his brain and his emotions were no longer in agreement was pretty damn disturbing.

Why the hell did he want Ferrara's attention now?

It made no sense.

Scowling, Nate forced himself to look away from his boss and pulled his phone out.

He texted Maya.

So I may have sucked his cock again. What do I do now?

Maya sent him a facepalm emoji.

Yeah. That about summed it up.

Chapter 13

Nate took a deep breath before entering Ferrara's office.

"You wanted to see me, sir?"

Ferrara lifted his gaze from his computer and simply eyed him for a moment.

"Close the door."

Nate's heart jumped into his throat—or at least it felt like it. "I'm not sucking you off again," he hissed. "Yesterday was a one-time-thing—"

"Close the door."

Nate closed the door, hating himself for the way his body seemed completely unable not to listen to this man's commands.

"We're leaving on a business trip tomorrow."

Nate blinked. That wasn't what he'd expected. "What?"

"We have received an excellent offer for a partnership with a European corporation. It'll open a new market for us in the UK, Switzerland, and Italy if the deal goes through."

Frowning, Nate studied the grim expression on Satan's face. "You don't exactly look happy about it."

"Ian was the one who normally dealt with that side of the business." Ferrara's lips thinned, his unseeing gaze on his computer. "But he can't leave his family now, so I'll have to deal with it."

Nate nodded.

He knew his boss preferred managing the video game publishing to everything else the Caldwell Group got involved in. Still, he was surprised by Ferrara's obvious reluctance—he usually wasn't one to complain about work, no matter what it entailed.

"What is the problem, exactly?"

"There is no problem."

Nate rolled his eyes. *Sure.* "Please. I know you."

Ferrara raised his eyebrows.

Resisting the urge to stick his tongue out, Nate corrected himself with, "I know you better than ninety-nine percent of people you come in contact with. So please don't insult my intelligence. This trip clearly bothers you. Why?"

"Even if Ian were available, my presence at the negotiations was requested specifically."

Okay, that was a little weird. But it still didn't entirely explain the grim look on Ferrara's face.

"And?" Nate said.

"The negotiations will take place in Italy."

Nate was beyond confused.

"And that's a problem why, exactly? Isn't it your home country? Surely you've been to Italy since moving to the US?"

"Of course. The location isn't a problem by itself. It's who the offer is coming from."

"All right, I'm completely lost now. Explain it to me like I'm stupid. Use small words."

"The offer is coming from OrbitaProm."

"That means nothing to me."

"Its CEO is Roman Demidov," Ferrara said, his gaze turning thoughtful.

"Again, that means nothing to me."

"Demidov is... well known in certain circles."

"Ugh," Nate said, beyond frustrated. "It's like pulling teeth! Can you elaborate for once instead of being all arrogant, mysterious, and shit?"

Satan shot him an irritated look, but to Nate's surprise, he actually clarified what he meant.

"He's a Russian oligarch suspected to be an important figure in the Russian mafia," he said, without any inflection in his voice. "Or maybe he used to be one. There have been rumors for the past few years that he's getting rid of the illegal side of his business, but I don't know how true the rumors are." The corners of his mouth turned downward. "I don't exactly move in those circles, so any information I have is secondhand and possibly unreliable."

Nate tried to digest what that meant—what Ferrara wasn't saying.

"You suspect Demidov has some nefarious motives? Because of your family?"

Ferrara shot him a sardonic look. "Have you been gossiping about me?"

Nate flushed. "No more than everyone else. It's common knowledge that your family is… you-know-what."

"You-know-what," the asshole repeated, his lips twitching.

Nate glowered at him. "Don't mock me. So what, you think he wants to use you to get to your family? Everyone knows your family basically disowned you."

A strange expression crossed Ferrara's face. He shrugged.

"Then what are you worried about?" Nate said.
"I'm not worried."
Nate rolled his eyes again.

"Right. What are you *mildly concerned* about then?"

Ferrara said nothing.

God, he was so damn infuriating!

Nate racked his mind. "You're worried he's made a deal with your father to get you implicated in something you don't want?"

After a few moments, Ferrara shrugged, his eyes hooded. "It's possible."

Nate was sure Ferrara wasn't telling him something important, but he doubted he'd get an honest answer—or any answer at all.

"You may leave early today to pack and get your things in order before the trip. Brenda has already bought the tickets. You can get more details about the trip from her."

"Why do you need me with you, exactly?" Nate said. "You didn't take me with you to the Japanese trip."

"Because I didn't need you."

"But now you need me? Why?"

"Later," Ferrara said curtly, returning his gaze to his computer. "Pack for a week-long trip."

Nate looked at him suspiciously, his Spidey-senses tingling and insisting that something was off, but he knew when he was being dismissed.

He turned and left, feeling baffled and annoyed.

***

"I don't like it," Maya said, watching Nate put his charger into his suitcase.

"I thought you had your own charger?" Nate said, looking around and trying to remember if he packed his toothbrush.

His sister sighed. "Don't play dumb. You know what I mean. I don't get why he needs you for this trip."

"I'm his assistant," Nate reminded her.

Maya humphed, looking as skeptical as Nate felt. "What will you be assisting him with during business negotiations at some fancy Italian mansion?"

Nate shrugged, trying not to show that he'd felt equally confused ever since he'd found out the details of the trip from Brenda—that they would be staying at Roman Demidov's luxurious villa on Lake Como for the duration of the negotiations.

"Lake Como sounds nice," he said lightly. "Maybe I'll visit that villa from Star Wars while I'm there. I've always wanted to see Italy but I didn't think it'd actually happen anytime soon—and free of charge."

Maya snorted. "Free? I'm sure you'll be earning it on your knees."

Nate glared at her, his face warming. "That's not—that's not why he's taking me with him! It isn't happening again."

"Right."

"It isn't!" Nate said, hating how defensive and weak his voice sounded, even though he was telling the truth. He was.

He grabbed his suitcase and headed out, too annoyed with Maya to say goodbye.

But she caught up with him outside. "Sorry, I was being an ass," she said, grabbing his arm and hugging him. "Have a nice trip, yeah?"

Nate nodded, dropping a kiss on her forehead.

She pulled back and looked him in the eyes, her gaze serious. "Just be careful, all right? I don't trust that man."

Nate could only smile faintly and nod.

He was almost late for boarding.

"Where have you been?" Ferrara said sharply when Nate entered the first-class cabin.

"I'm here, aren't I?" Nate said, dropping himself into the seat next to his boss. His stomach clenched as he caught Ferrara's dark eyes. He looked away quickly.

Maya was wrong, right? *Right?*

He looked down, acutely aware of the man beside him. "My sister thinks you're taking me with you to suck your cock."

Someone made a choking noise.

Nate flushed, realizing that there was someone else in the cabin—an elderly woman in the seat by the opposite window. She was glaring at him, clearly scandalized.

Nate shifted his gaze away from her to his boss, whose eyebrows were quirked.

"You gossip about me with your sister," he said. "I'm flattered."

"Oh, fuck you. So is she right?" He lowered his voice, mindful of the old woman. "Because I'm serious: I'm not sucking your cock again."

"Your sister is wrong," Ferrara said.

Nate gave him a suspicious look. "You have to admit it's pretty weird that you're taking me with you on what is essentially a vacation in one of the most beautiful places on the planet."

"It will hardly be a vacation. The negotiations will involve seven executives of seven different companies. They're just being held in an informal setting."

Nate narrowed his eyes. He was hiding something. Nate could feel it.

"And are all of those execs bringing their PAs with them?"

"I would hardly know, would I?"

When Nate just gave him another suspicious look, Ferrara sighed. "Fine," he said. "I'm taking you with me for a very specific reason. But it has nothing to do with making you suck my cock."

"What reason?"

"Roman Demidov is in a relationship with a man. Making him think that I'm like him would make it easier to build rapport with him and—"

"Wait, what?" Nate said. "You want us to pretend we're in a relationship?"

Ferrara shot him a rather pinched look. The plane started moving. "When you put it that way, yes."

Nate laughed.

Ferrara's expression shifted into one of annoyance. "What's so amusing?"

Nate just laughed harder. "You—in a relationship—with me!" He laughed so hard his ribs started hurting, but he couldn't stop. It was the most ridiculous thing he'd ever heard.

"Stop. Laughing."

The look of supreme irritation on Ferrara's face just made Nate laugh harder.

He stopped laughing only when he felt the plane pick up the speed.

Oh, fuck.

His amusement was gone so fast, it gave him whiplash.

Nate swallowed, looking at the scenery passing by, faster and faster. His stomach tied into knots, his palms feeling clammy.

"You look green. Don't tell me you're afraid of flying."

"I don't—I didn't know," Nate croaked out, trying to ignore the way the plane trembled. "This is my first time on a plane."

Ferrara stared at him incredulously before cursing in Italian.

They were about to take off. They were about to leave the safe, sweet ground and become a giant tin full of people flying in the sky—

"For fuck's sake," Ferrara muttered, and grabbed his trembling hand. "Breathe. Calm down. That's an order."

Nate breathed, staring at the strong, darker hand gripping his pale hand. Ferrara wasn't gentle at all. But it was fine. His strength was reassuring. His insufferable bossiness was familiar and—god help him—*comforting*.

His hand was warm, dry, and firm.

Nate focused on it, on the calluses he could feel, on the subtle, familiar scent of Ferrara's aftershave.

He breathed.

It was fine. It would be fine. Millions of people traveled by plane every day. Nothing happened to them. He was being silly.

"It's never going to work," he managed, trying to distract himself from the fact that they were going to be thousands of feet in the sky. "Your plan is ridiculous."

"And why is that?" Ferrara said, gripping Nate's hand harder as the plane took off.

Fuck, it took off.

They were airborne.

"Because..." Nate swallowed. *Breathe*. "Because they'll never buy it."

"Why not?"

Nate chuckled distractedly.

They were higher and higher, the clouds the only thing visible now.

He breathed deeper, taking a lungful of his boss's scent. "Because you don't even do relationships. You have no idea how they work. And you and me?" He chuckled again, meeting Ferrara's dark eyes. "It's just ridiculous. No one will buy it."

Ferrara didn't look fazed. "You weren't wrong when you claimed that you know me better than ninety-nine percent of people. I don't see why they wouldn't buy it."

Trying to ignore the disgustingly pleased feeling caused by Ferrara's words, Nate shook his head. "I can claim that I know you better than most people do, but that actually doesn't mean much, because you don't let people close. Couples have a certain intimacy in their interactions—"

"You have sucked my cock," Ferrara said flatly. "It doesn't get much more intimate than that."

Nate scowled at him. "I'm not talking about that kind of intimacy. Sex doesn't equal emotional intimacy. You should know that better than anyone."

Ferrara shrugged, conceding his point. "Then what do you mean?"

"People in relationships... they touch each other outside of sex—"

"You touch me all the time. In fact, you're touching me right now."

Nate glared at him, but he had to admit Ferrara did have a point. As his PA, Nate was used to touching him and being manhandled by Ferrara all the time.

"Still," he grumbled. "People in relationships smile at each other and stuff."

"Your arguments are getting more illogical by the minute," Ferrara said, *smiling* condescendingly.

Asshole.

"Your superior smiles don't count!" Nate argued, playing with Ferrara's fingers absentmindedly as he tried to come up with better arguments. How could he not see that it was a terrible, ridiculous idea?

"People in a relationship kiss!" he finally said.

Ferrara's forehead wrinkled. "No one would expect me to kiss you in front of everyone during serious business negotiations. That would be just tasteless and immature."

Nate had to admit he was right. "Still," he said. "I don't like lying to people."

"You wouldn't have to lie to anyone. Just keep your mouth shut, stick close to me, and smile. It's not hard."

Nate frowned. "And that's all I'll have to do? You promise?"

Something shifted in Ferrara's expression.

Nate tensed up. "You are not telling me something."

"It would be helpful if you build good rapport with Luke Whitford, Demidov's lover," Ferrara said at last, clearly carefully choosing his words. "He will likely be more honest and straightforward than Demidov."

"Why me? Why can't you do it yourself?"

"He won't talk to me. But you… everyone talks to you. You seem—honest."

"Honest?" Nate said, torn between laughing and rolling his eyes. He settled on doing both.

"Kind," Ferrara said, looking like he'd swallowed a lemon. "Friendly."

Nate snorted. "Right. No one would call you kind or friendly. So what, you want me to spy for you?"

The look Ferrara gave him was distinctly unamused. "Not spy. Just do your usual thing. Smile. Look approachable and friendly. Steer the conversation toward Demidov and me. I hear Luke Whitford is pretty talkative."

"But wouldn't Demidov know that you're actually straight? You've never been seen with a man."

Ferrara shook his head. "It doesn't mean anything. Demidov allegedly dated only women too until his relationship with his Englishman."

"You have an answer for everything, don't you?" Nate said with a sigh. He didn't know why he'd even bothered to argue—his demon of a boss never changed his mind once he made a decision.

"Fine," Nate said, leaning back in his seat and closing his eyes.

His hand was still in Ferrara's when he fell asleep.

Chapter 14

Roman Demidov's villa was breathtaking.

They arrived just as the sun was setting over Lake Como, and Nate stopped, in awe of the sheer beauty of it. The water glittered like diamonds as it reflected the sunset, and the tall mountains surrounding the picturesque lake made him feel incredibly small. "Damn," he whispered, all the tiredness after the transatlantic flight gone.

He turned his head and found Ferrara looking at the lake with a very strange expression, his hands in the pockets of his suit pants. Was that wistfulness in his gaze?

"Did you miss it?" Nate said before he could stop himself.

"America has beautiful places, too," Ferrara said without any inflection in his voice.

"But it isn't home," Nate said quietly.

Ferrara said nothing.

Nate eyed his hard profile. He hadn't missed the shift in his boss's mood ever since they'd landed in Milan. There was something... *different* about him, in the way he held himself. Even his voice sounded a little softer, more melodic when he spoke in Italian, and Nate found himself fascinated, wishing he understood the language.

There was another difference—and one that unnerved Nate a little.

Two bodyguards in dark suits were now following them everywhere, their faces grim and blank.

It made Nate feel a little jumpy and ridiculous, as if he'd ended up in some gangster movie. Ferrara barely seemed to notice them, completely ignoring their presence.

When Nate grabbed his suitcase, Ferrara said shortly, "Leave it. Alessio and Paolo will take care of our baggage." Then he laid his hand on Nate's nape and steered him toward the beautiful villa.

Two men emerged out of the house.

The older man was about Ferrara's height and age, or maybe a little older, his blue eyes assessing and sharp as they flicked between him and Ferrara.

"Welcome," he said, his voice neutral as he stretched his hand out for Nate to shake. "Roman Demidov."

Nate shook his hand, a little surprised that he was being greeted first. He'd thought he'd just be ignored. "Nate Parrish," he said, shooting a confused look at his boss.

Ferrara's face betrayed nothing, his hand still on Nate's nape, heavy and familiar.

"We weren't aware you were bringing someone," Demidov said in the same carefully neutral tone, his gaze shifting to Ferrara.

He finally shook his hand.

"Is that a problem?" Ferrara said, his voice equally reserved.

"Not at all!" said the guy beside Demidov, his British accent obvious. "The more, the merrier." He was a young man, likely in his early twenties, with a mop of curly, dark gold hair that made him look even younger than he probably was. He was dressed kind of flamboyantly, his floral shirt and shorts a stark contrast next to Demidov's blue dress shirt and dark pants.

The guy gave Nate a friendly smile. "I'm Luke

Whitford, by the way. It's just... It's a pretty small villa—there isn't a free room for you I'm afraid. All the other guests have already arrived and they've taken all the best rooms."

"It's not a problem," Ferrara said before Nate could say anything, putting his hand back on Nate's neck, his touch more caressing than it normally was.

Nate barely stopped himself from flinching. He smiled faintly, his face becoming warm when an expression of understanding appeared on Luke's face.

"Great, then," Luke said, exchanging a quick look with Demidov before turning back to them. "Come on, let me show you your room. Your bodyguards can stay in the security house with our bodyguards."

"They'll stay outside our room," Ferrara stated.

Luke shook his head with a sunny smile. "Sorry, but no men with guns are allowed into the house. My house, my rules." He looked Ferrara in the eyes, his gaze becoming serious. "Look, I... understand why you might be cautious, but I give you my word. You don't need bodyguards here."

After a long moment, Ferrara looked from Luke to Demidov. The Russian gave a clipped nod, something rueful about his expression. "He took away even my gun."

Luke smiled and pecked him on the cheek quickly. "It's for your own good, Roma."

Taking their suitcases from the bodyguards, Nate and Ferrara followed Luke into the house.

Nate barely paid attention to Luke's tour through the villa, still reeling from the surreality of it all. Fuck, what was he doing here, among these filthy rich people who owned villas on Lake Como and talked about stuff like bodyguards and guns as if it were completely normal?

"The room is a bit small," Luke said apologetically, pushing a door open.

Nate nearly laughed when they entered the spacious bedroom with a stunning lakeview. A bit small, his ass.

"It's fine," he said with a faint smile, trying not to stare at the king-sized bed that dominated the room.

"You're probably tired. I'll let you rest. We've already had supper, but if you're hungry, just push this button—the maids can bring you something to eat."

"Thank you."

When the door closed behind Luke, Ferrara walked around the room, his gaze sharp. Searching.

"What are you doing?" Nate said, following him with his eyes.

"I doesn't look like there are cameras here."

Nate let out a laugh. "Seriously? We aren't in a Bond movie."

Ferrara sighed, shrugging out of his suit jacket. "You'd be surprised how many businessmen use those methods in real life. Corporate espionage is a thing."

"I wouldn't know," Nate said, reading between the lines. Normal businessmen might not use such methods, but Roman Demidov had a very sketchy reputation. It was probably smart to be careful even though they had nothing to hide—besides the fact that they weren't really in a relationship.

He looked at the bed again and his stomach did a little flip-flop.

He was being ridiculous. The bed was big enough for four people. They could share it without touching each other. It wouldn't be an issue.

"They seem like a great couple," Nate said, just to say something.

Ferrara made a derisive sound, unbuttoning his shirt. "A strange one. They couldn't be more different."

"You wouldn't recognize a good relationship if it smacked you in the face," Nate said, opening Ferrara's suitcase. Then he stopped. It wasn't his fucking job to unpack his boss's clothes. He wasn't actually his manservant. Or wife.

Nate scowled, rubbing the back of his very warm neck.

He opened his own suitcase and grabbed a t-shirt and a pair of boxers. "I'm going to shower first," he said, feeling—and probably sounding—incredibly awkward. He wasn't even sure why. He just felt on edge, his skin tingling, too tight, too *something*.

He glanced back at Ferrara, who was unbuckling his belt, already shirtless.

Dark eyes met his.

Swallowing, Nate turned away and strode to the ensuite.

Chapter 15

Sharing a bed with his boss was somehow the single weirdest thing he'd ever done, and that said a lot.

Nate stared at the strips of moonlight on the ceiling and breathed evenly, trying to will himself to fall asleep.

It didn't work.

He was acutely aware of the man beside him, of his steady breaths and the heat he exuded. It was a good thing the room wasn't hot, a fresh cool breeze coming through the open window.

"You're hot," Nate complained.

Ferrara made a strangled sort of sound, something between a laugh and a sigh. "Thanks," he said, his voice extremely dry.

Nate flushed, realizing how that had sounded. "Shut up. You're literally very warm."

"I run hot. I'm not used to sleeping in clothes."

Now that was something Nate really hadn't needed to know. "And you're wearing clothes for my sake? I didn't know you even understood the concept of doing something for someone else's sake."

"You're right." The other man sat up and pulled his t-shirt off. "I shouldn't have bothered. It's not like you haven't seen me naked."

Whoa.

"I *haven't* seen you naked," Nate said quickly, looking away, even though he couldn't see much in the dark. "I've seen parts of you. Naked. But not all of you!"

"You had my cock in your mouth," Ferrara said. "Seeing my ankles shouldn't make you faint."

Nate squeezed his eyes shut. He could still hear Ferrara lie back in the bed with a satisfied sigh.

"Stop reminding me of it."

"Of what?" Satan said. "Of having my cock in your mouth?"

"Stop saying that." Nate bit the inside of his cheek, trying to think very unsexy thoughts.

It didn't work.

His thoughts kept fixating on Ferrara's cock. Inches away from him. Probably half-hard at the very least, considering how horny Satan always was. Thick and long, standing tall between Ferrara's muscular thighs, the cockhead fat and red and glistening with pre-come.

Nate's mouth watered. God, he needed to distract himself, before he could do something he would regret.

Nate searched for something to say. "Why did you leave Italy?"

"What makes you think I'll tell you?" Ferrara said, but his tone was mild, almost soft.

Sensing a prime opportunity to actually get some answers, Nate opened his eyes and stared at the ceiling again. "Let's play a game. You'll honestly answer my question and then I'll answer yours, and so on. If one of us doesn't want to answer the question, he owes the other a hundred thousand dollars."

"You don't have a hundred thousand dollars."

"I'm an open book," Nate said with a smile, very pleased with himself for coming up with such an ingenious idea. Either he'd finally get some answers, or he'd be rich by the end of the night. Win-win. "I have nothing to hide, so I'm not going to need it."

After a moment, Ferrara said, "Fine."

It made Nate a little wary. Was there something Ferrara actually wanted to know about him? Something he wouldn't want to answer?

"You first," Nate said. "Why did you leave Italy? It's obvious that you love it. There had to be a reason."

He heard the other man exhale.

"There isn't a single reason. There were a few reasons that contributed to my decision."

"Come on, that's not an answer."

Ferrara was silent for so long Nate started thinking he wasn't going to tell him, but finally, he broke the silence. "My uncle was shot in front me when I was nine," he said, his voice quiet and so carefully toneless it didn't sound natural. "My father has barely survived countless assassination attempts. That life… it isn't as glamorous and fun as Hollywood makes it out to be. You have to constantly watch your back. You can't even step out of the house without bodyguards. It drove me up the wall. I felt caged. I was utterly fed up by the time I was eighteen. I wanted out. And I got out."

Nate frowned. He almost regretted asking the question now. He didn't want to understand his boss or sympathize with him. He was also a little confused. Olivia had told him that Ferrara's family had kicked him out. But then again, Ferrara leaving the family business likely hadn't endeared him to his family. Maybe they were pissed off enough to refuse to pay ransom for him. "You said there wasn't just one reason."

"You're like a dog with a bone," Ferrara said, a hint of amusement appearing in his voice. "Yes, there were other reasons. Less important reasons."

"Like what?"

"It doesn't matter."

"You promised an honest answer."

"An honest answer isn't the same as a full answer. Technically I did answer your question."

Nate glowered at him in the dark.

The bastard laughed. "I can practically see the face you're making right now."

Nate turned onto his side and poked at Ferrara's ribs with his finger, hard. "Give me a full answer or that's a hundred thousand dollars you owe me and I'm not answering any of your questions."

Ferrara caught his hand and forced him to stop poking at his ribs. But instead of letting go of it, he just put Nate's hand on his stomach.

Nate's fingers twitched against the hard muscle and warm skin. He should probably remove his hand. But… it wasn't doing anything. It was just laid on his boss's abs. There was nothing weird about it, right?

"As far as I can remember, there have always been half-naked women in our house," Ferrara said, his voice neutral once again. "When I was a kid, I didn't know it wasn't normal, and didn't understand that there was a correlation between the half-naked women and my mother falling asleep with a wine bottle."

He didn't say anything else, but Nate could read between the lines. A cheating father and a depressed, alcoholic mother would make anyone want to leave such a toxic household. Coupled with the assassination attempts, bodyguards, and the immense pressure… Nate felt a reluctant pang of sympathy.

He chewed on his lip, stroking Ferrara's happy trail absentmindedly. "Is that why you don't do relationships? Because you didn't see a good example of it growing up?"

"That's two questions, not one. Shouldn't it be your turn?"

"I'll answer two questions if you answer this one." Nate wasn't sure why it was suddenly so important, but he just *wanted* to know. He wanted to know everything about this man, what made him tick, what had shaped him into the man he was now. It was probably a little messed-up how much he liked learning things about a man he couldn't stand, but Nate had come to accept it. This man messed him up, period.

Ferrara gave a soft snort. "The answer isn't interesting. I don't do relationships because I've never met anyone who made me want to be monogamous. I don't think that woman even exists, so I have no intention of making some poor woman miserable when I inevitably cheat on her."

"Careful, you almost sound like a nice person," Nate said with a smile. "All right, my turn! Ask away."

Ferrara hummed and fell silent for a while.

It made Nate nervous. He tried to think of the worst question Ferrara could possibly ask. Fuck, what if he asked if Nate liked sucking his cock?

"Do you really hate working under me?"

Nate's mind immediately went to the gutter. In his defense, Ferrara was fucking *naked* beside him; it was totally understandable that he had imagined being physically under him, which... He pushed the image away, his face uncomfortably warm. God, what the hell was wrong with him?

Running a hand over his warm cheeks, Nate cleared his throat a little. He opened his mouth to say that of course he hated it, but then he paused.

That would be a lie.

He couldn't deny that he felt invigorated being back at work, which didn't make sense, considering that there was nothing invigorating about the job of a PA.

"It's not exactly the job of my dreams," Nate said. "And you're a horrible boss. Like, you're so horrible I sometimes vividly imagine choking you with your own tie."

"That's not an answer."

Of course it had been too much to hope that Satan wouldn't notice that he was evading a straight answer.

"I don't hate working for you anymore," Nate said stiffly, tightening his grip. "I don't like it, either." He cleared his throat again, and said, desperate to switch the subject, "All right, second question. Go ahead." Surely any other question would be less uncomfortable than this one.

"Are you going to jerk me off or not? All this fondling is just frustrating."

Nate froze. Then, two things registered at the same time. His hand was on Ferrara's hard cock, fondling it absentmindedly. His own cock was hard, too.

Fuck.

Nate snatched his hand away, his face *burning*. What the hell, he had no idea when he'd even started groping him!

"I was distracted by the conversation," he said, wiping his hand off on the sheets. It did nothing to erase the feel of the warm, hard cock he'd just been touching. "I'm not responsible for my subconscious!"

Ferrara chuckled, but didn't say anything. Thank fuck for small mercies.

Nate turned away and stared at the wall, feeling so confused and mortified. If he couldn't even trust himself, who could he trust?

Chapter 16

By the time Nate returned from his walk along the lakeshore, he was resolved to act like last night's embarrassing incident hadn't happened. Nate had been relieved to find Ferrara gone when he woke up in the morning, but now it felt like the longer he put their confrontation off, the worse it would be. It was time to man up and face the music. He could hardly avoid his boss all day long, every day. Besides, he was kind of curious how the talks were going.

It was easy to find where everyone was—he only had to follow the noise.

Around fifteen people were lounging by the pool in various state of undress, mostly men but a few women too. They all were clearly buzzed, laughing and chattering, their eyes a little glassy. Apparently, "business negotiations in an informal setting" involved lots of booze and weed and not much business.

Nate's gaze was immediately drawn to his boss.

Ferrara was stretched out in a lounge chair, his big body seemingly relaxed, but his black eyes were as alert and sharp as ever as he nursed his beer. His white shirt was unbuttoned, but otherwise he was mostly dressed. The nearest lounge chair was occupied by Roman Demidov, who had Luke in his lap. Luke was laughing about something and gesticulating animatedly while Demidov looked at Luke with a small, indulgent smile on his face.

He was the only one besides Ferrara who seemed completely sober.

Ferrara's gaze found Nate's, his expression unreadable, before he motioned with his head slightly. *Come here.*

Nate hesitated, wondering what he expected him to do, exactly. All the chairs were occupied. Was he supposed to stand there awkwardly while Ferrara lounged in his chair?

The more he thought about it, the more annoyed he became. If Ferrara hadn't insinuated that they were together, he wouldn't feel so awkward and out of his comfort zone now. It pissed him off that the asshole looked so relaxed and arrogant while Nate was anything but.

Maybe it was time to push *Ferrara* out of his comfort zone for once.

Glancing back at Luke, who was half-sprawled on top of Demidov, Nate smiled. Maybe it was a crazy idea, but what the hell, wasn't that what Ferrara had brought him here for?

With new determination, Nate strode toward his boss, smiling. His smile probably looked a little deranged, judging by the sudden wariness that appeared in Ferrara's body language.

Yep, he was so doing it.

Nate plopped down onto Ferrara's lap and looped his arms around his neck. "Hey there, handsome." So he had totally stolen the line from Ferrara's booty calls; sue him.

Ferrara stared at him blankly, his body tense under him.

Nate smiled wider. "I missed you," he said, loudly enough for Demidov and Luke to hear. "What have you been up to?"

Without waiting for a response, he pressed his mouth against Ferrara's firm lips, barely suppressing a laugh. Fuck, this was hilarious. Why hadn't he thought of this sooner?

He felt the other man stiffen even further before an arm suddenly wrapped around him and pulled him closer.

And then Ferrara was kissing him.

Kissing him. For real.

Nate's mind went utterly blank, unable to comprehend what was happening. The kiss was thought-annihilating, it was debilitating—Nate felt like he was in free fall. He'd never been kissed like that, with such control and forcefulness. It made him feel shaky and unsure, out of control and off balance. Ferrara's mouth was so damn confident, he even kissed with arrogance, the dick, his tongue pushing into Nate's mouth as if he owned it. It pissed Nate off—it pissed him off that he was allowing it, meekly accepting the kisses and just gasping, overwhelmed and confused, as his Satan of a boss plundered his mouth with domineering, bruising kisses.

When Ferrara finally let his mouth go, Nate could only blink owlishly at him, out of breath, his thoughts in chaos. He licked his lips. They felt sensitive and tender—his whole chin did from Ferrara's stubble.

The asshole smiled and said, "I missed you, too, bello."

Nate glared at him.

***

So. That was apparently a thing now. A new game they had been playing the whole afternoon.

Nate wondered glumly how they had come to this.

This being the fact that he was sprawled in Ferrara's lap, eating strawberries out of his boss's hands.

But he was determined not to lose, no matter how weirded out he was by the entire situation.

Nate smiled at Ferrara and licked his fingers as he accepted the strawberry into his mouth. Ferrara's dark eyes watched it—watched his mouth—a little too fixatedly for that to be just an act. The asshole was probably imagining stuffing his cock into his mouth. Nate was aware that Ferrara was aroused—it would have been hard to miss, considering that Nate was in his goddamn *lap*—but the bastard was always somewhat horny, so Nate didn't take it personally.

Ferrara leaned in and captured his mouth again. Ugh, not again. Nate's eyelids slipped shut, no matter how hard he fought to keep them open. Fuck, it was unbearable, being kissed by this man—overwhelming, wrong, and just too much. It left Nate feeling shaky and meek, like a stranger. No matter how many times he told himself that he'd take control over the kiss, he could never quite do it, just opening his mouth passively and letting himself be kissed within an inch of his life.

A sound slipped out of his throat when Ferrara pulled away. It *wasn't* a whine. He hated Ferrara and he hated his horrible kisses that made him feel like a different person altogether.

"You kiss terribly," Ferrara murmured before gripping his chin harder and kissing him again.

"You kiss terribly, too," Nate said when he was allowed to breathe again. He hated how shaky his voice sounded, how hard it was to concentrate on anything but Ferrara's face. He wasn't even sure if the other people were watching them—if they were still even there.

The rest of the world just seemed fuzzy around the edges, distant and bizarre, Ferrara's sun-bronzed face the only thing in focus, those black, intense eyes holding him in some weird spell.

Someone coughed slightly.

Nate blinked and dragged his eyes away from Ferrara. It took him a moment to focus his gaze on Luke, who was looking at them with a knowing little smile.

"The dinner is ready," Luke said. "Everyone is already hanging out at the beach patio. Let's go. Or do you need a moment?"

Realizing what he was implying, Nate flushed and scrambled off Ferrara's lap. No, they definitely didn't need a moment, thank you very much.

He felt more than saw Ferrara get up and follow them. Nate walked faster, catching up to Luke and walking side by side with him. His body felt too warm, his nape prickling with awareness. His lips were tingling and sore from all the kissing, and he pursed them, trying to get rid of the feeling of Ferrara's mouth on them. It didn't work.

"So," Luke said, breaking the silence. "How long have you been together? Not too long, right?"

Nate looked at the guy, unsure what to say. Ferrara was on the phone, speaking in a low voice behind them, so he was no help.

"What makes you think so?" he said evasively, hoping to avoid a direct answer. He didn't want to contradict whatever Ferrara had told them while Nate was on a walk.

Luke grinned, looking so damn pretty and youthful that Nate had an uncomfortable thought that he might be jailbait. But surely Demidov wouldn't date someone underage, right?

"It's just obvious that you're still at the 'Does he or doesn't he?' stage, when everything is still new and exciting and a little weird." Luke's expression turned wistful. "I remember that—I remember getting shivery and tingly from Roman's every touch."

"And now you don't?" Nate said, trying to shift the conversation to a less uncomfortable topic.

Luke smiled a little. "Oh, I absolutely do. But now it feels weird when he *isn't* touching me. I've just moved on from the infatuation phase to the 'he's my home' phase. You'll get there, too."

Nate almost laughed at that. Luke was horrible at reading people.

"So you've been together for a while?" Nate said, steering the conversation back toward Luke. "You aren't... You aren't actually all that young, then?"

Chuckling, Luke shook his head. "I'm pretty sure I'm older than you are, mate. Don't let my baby face fool you. Roman and I have been together for years."

Before Nate could say anything, they reached the beautiful patio on the lakefront. Dinner was being served there, and the other guests were already helping themselves to the delicious food.

Nate's stomach growled, very loudly—he hadn't eaten anything besides a few strawberries since the morning. He flushed in embarrassment, but Luke gave him an understanding look. "I know, I could eat a horse right now."

Demidov smiled, pulling his lover into the seat next to him. "I've tried horse meat in Uzbekistan. It was surprisingly tasty. You should try it sometime."

"Don't be gross, Roma," Luke said, pulling a face, which only made Demidov laugh.

After a moment's hesitation, Nate sat down too and started filling his plate. He studiously ignored it when he felt Ferrara take the empty seat beside him.

"Pass me the salt," Ferrara said.

Nate passed him the salt without looking at him.

He stabbed a piece of chicken on his plate and put it in his mouth. Chewed. Ferrara shifted beside him. Nate poured himself some juice. Drank it.

Ferrara sighed. "Stop being ridiculous," he said quietly, just for Nate's ears.

"I'm not doing anything," Nate said, still not looking at him.

"I didn't think a few kisses would finally shut you up."

A few kisses? More like dozens of kisses.

"Oh what, you would have done it months ago?" Nate said snidely.

"Here you are," Ferrara said, sounding satisfied, the prick. It confirmed Nate's old suspicion that Ferrara found his bitching entertaining and it was the only reason he tolerated it.

"It was your idea," Ferrara murmured.

Yeah, don't remind me. He hated that it always turned out that way: Nate always thought he could finally outplay his boss, get the upper hand, but Ferrara always managed to adapt superbly and turn the tables. Even now he looked completely at ease already, as if Nate hadn't stunned him with his kiss.

Nate scowled and focused on his food, resolved to ignore his insufferable boss.

But fuck, it was impossible. His senses were hyperaware of everything Ferrara did, his ears straining to hear his conversation with the woman to his right.

They were conversing in low tones, the woman smiling widely and playing with her hair as she looked Ferrara in the eyes.

Nate pursed his lips, a little annoyed. Of course he and Ferrara weren't actually a real couple, but the woman didn't know that. Why the hell was she flirting with a supposedly taken man while Nate was right there? It was utterly shameless. And it was utterly shameless the way her dark eyes kept roaming over Ferrara's muscular chest—the asshole hadn't bothered to button his shirt up. Show-off. It wasn't that hot in the evening, the weather was perfectly pleasant.

Well, Nate should probably take issue with their flirting, right? If they were a real couple, he wouldn't have let someone else flirt with his partner so shamelessly. In fact, it would probably be weird if he *didn't* put an end to this.

"Raffaele," Nate said. He paused, the name feeling weird on his tongue. He'd never called his boss that even in his thoughts. Never allowed himself.

Ferrara turned his head, something like surprise flickering in his eyes. Maybe he was as startled by the use of his first name as Nate was. "Yes?" he said.

Nate brushed his fingers over the other man's chest before slowly buttoning up his shirt. "You're being rude, babe," he said sharply, trying to sound jealous. It was easy. Much easier than he'd expected. Maybe his acting skills were better than he'd thought. "You should have told this very nice woman that you're taken before she could get her hopes up."

The black eyes just gazed at him for a moment before Ferrara's lips curled a little. "There's no need to be jealous," he said, leaning in and kissing him on the lips.

It was a chaste, brief kiss, perfectly appropriate for an informal dinner outdoors. But Nate's mind went utterly empty with that horrible *dizziness-submissiveness* again. He parted his lips, his hands gripping Ferrara's shirt. *Please don't. Please don't stop.* He was chasing Ferrara's mouth with his own, Nate realized with a sinking feeling, but he couldn't stop. He needed—he needed—

He whined when Ferrara pulled back. Fucking *whined*. It was mortifying.

Ferrara studied him, his gaze so very dark. Bottomless. Nate had never known what it meant to drown in someone's eyes until that moment. It wasn't a pleasant feeling. Nate couldn't breathe. He couldn't *think*. He could only look at him helplessly, dazed and lost.

Ferrara grabbed Nate's arm and practically dragged him away from the table.

Nate let him, his mind hazy and his knees weak.

There was a small building nearby, some kind of kitchen used by the staff.

Ferrara dragged him behind it.

He let go of Nate's arm and looked at Nate with his black, demonic eyes.

The moment stretched, the tension unbearable.

"Kneel," he said, voice deep and low.

As if in a dream, Nate dropped to his knees.

He sucked him off right there, not giving a damn that they were just a few feet away from other people. All he wanted was this cock in his mouth, the heady, musky taste of it, the feel of it, the thickness stretching his lips. Fuck, it felt so good, the hands in his hair, bossy and demanding, the cock moving in his mouth.

It felt just right.

But he wanted more.

As though hearing his thoughts, Ferrara started thrusting, fucking his mouth in earnest. Nate moaned around the cock and fumbled with his own fly. Pulling out his own erection, he stroked it, hard and fast, while his boss used his mouth.

"Look at you," Ferrara said huskily. "You're the biggest cock slut I've ever seen."

The filthy words caused a horrible mix of arousal and humiliation, and Nate came, moaning around the cock in him. Ferrara groaned and slammed his cock against his throat a few times before spilling deep into it. Nate swallowed greedily, every single drop.

And he wanted more.

Jesus.

What had this man turned him into?

Chapter 17

Nate couldn't look Luke in the eye when he went downstairs for breakfast. He had been so eager to escape the bedroom before Ferrara could wake up that he hadn't considered that he'd have to face people who saw them leave yesterday and likely could guess what they had been doing behind the kitchen building.

Fuck, he'd never felt so embarrassed in his life.

Thankfully it was just Luke in the breakfast room. "Everyone else is probably nursing a hangover," Luke said, answering his unasked question. "Roman doesn't drink, but he likes sleeping in when he doesn't have to get up. I kept him up half the night." Luke smiled, a knowing look appearing on his face. "You've probably been up for a while, too, right?"

Ugh. Nate now understood the expression about wanting the ground to open up and swallow you, and he fervently wished for just that.

"Yeah," he said with a forced smile. How could he say that they weren't like that, that what happened yesterday hadn't been supposed to happen—again? How could he say that Raffaele Ferrara just had a terrible, horrible, no good, very bad effect on his body and brain? That he had sucked Nate's willpower and rational thoughts right through his mouth, like some kind of Dementor?

"You look well rested, though," Luke said, changing the subject, to Nate's relief. "You like it here?"

Nate nodded and tucked in. He did feel well rested. To his surprise, he'd fallen asleep as soon as his head had hit the pillow yesterday and he slept like a baby. It must have been the air. In fact, he had slept so well that he'd woken up with his face smothered against Ferrara's bare chest. Clearly his sleeping self was an idiot with no sense of self-preservation.

"It's lovely here," he said honestly when the silence stretched.

Before he could say anything else, Ferrara walked into the room, his eyes still heavy-lidded from sleep.

Nate pressed his lips together; even his ears turned hot. *Kneel*, Ferrara's low, commanding voice sounded in his head. Fuck, he couldn't believe he'd done it, just like that.

"Morning," he forced out, since it would be strange if he didn't say anything.

"Good morning," Luke said, too, looking at Ferrara curiously.

Ferrara didn't even look at him, his sleepy gaze fixed on Nate. "My coffee," he stated.

Nate glared at him. Had he forgotten that they weren't at the office?

"Get it yourself, babe," he said with his sweetest smile.

Dark eyes blinked slowly before their owner must have realized that this attitude was inappropriate in front of their captive audience. "It always tastes better when you make it," he said.

Nate nearly snorted.

Nice save.

But he did get up and walk to the table by the wall. It had everything anyone would need to make coffee just the way they wanted it.

"Do you need help?" a maid asked him, her accent heavy.

Nate shook his head. He didn't bother telling the girl that Ferrara was a grumpy dick in the morning and liked his coffee to be made in a very particular way. Nate didn't trust her to get it right.

By the time he returned with Ferrara's coffee, Roman Demidov had joined them. Ferrara accepted the coffee without as much as a glance at Nate, his attention on Demidov. They were talking business, so Nate went back to his seat and tried not to scowl into his own coffee.

"You're very comfortable with each other already," Luke said in a quiet voice, stirring his tea. "But if you want his attention, ask for it. Roman can get ridiculously busy and distracted by his work, too. The key is not to let work dominate your life."

Nate sipped his coffee. "I don't want his attention," he said. He *didn't*.

The look Luke shot him was so skeptical that Nate wished he could tell the guy that their supposed relationship was totally fake and having Satan's attention was the worst thing anyone could wish for.

He said neither of those things.

"Don't want to be too clingy?" Luke said with an understanding look. "I don't think he minds. You were the first thing he looked at when he entered the room. I'm not sure he even noticed me."

Nate made a noncommittal noise, marveling at Luke's poor observational skills.

"You make a lovely couple." Luke hesitated and then lowered his voice. "I honestly wasn't sure about Roman inviting Ferrara here because of…"

Nate looked back at him, curious.

"Because of his family?" he said, just as quietly.

Luke eyed him in an assessing manner. He must have found what he was looking for, because he eventually replied, "Yes. You've probably heard the rumors about Roman, right?"

Nate nodded. "Raffaele told me," he said, managing not to trip over the name this time.

"That makes things easier, I guess," Luke said with a rueful smile.

"You were against inviting Raffaele?"

"I was. It's nothing personal, you understand. I just didn't want to have anyone from Roman's past in our home—and that part of his life is in the past. But Roman can be so stubborn. He eventually talked me into it." He blushed slightly, and Nate got a sneaking suspicion what "talking into it" entailed.

"Why?" Nate said, looking at Luke curiously. Hopefully for once his "kind face" would do its job and make Luke confide in him.

Luke chewed on his bottom lip, something hesitant about his expression. "Roman has mostly shut down that side of his business," he said at last, his tone careful. "But an old... business partner in Italy is giving him trouble over it. He doesn't understand that no means no."

Translation: Roman Demidov's former criminal associates didn't want to be former associates.

Nate frowned. "And why does he need F—Raffaele? Because of his family connections? But he's estranged from his family."

His face flashing with a conspiratorial smile, Luke said, "Is he, really?"

"Yes," Nate said carefully. "Don't you know that his family refused to pay ransom for him when someone kidnapped him a decade ago?"

Amusement flashed in Luke's eyes. "That was very clever of him," he said, glancing at Ferrara. "Even Roman thought the kidnapping was real. We know that it was staged only because we found about it when we went through my father's files."

Staged?

"I'm not sure what you're talking about," Nate said faintly.

Luke peered at him before his eyes widened in something like bewilderment. "Oh, you really had no idea? I thought he'd tell you… You need to talk to him about it, then. Secrets are bad for a relationship."

Nate could only nod. He got to his feet, walked to Ferrara, and touched his arm. "I need to talk to you."

A deep wrinkle appeared between Ferrara's brows at the interruption.

He looked at Nate's hand for a moment before looking back at Nate's face.

At last, he got to his feet and Nate quickly turned and headed out of the room before Ferrara could lay a hand on his nape.

Nate led him to the library, shut the door and turned to him. "Luke implied that you aren't actually estranged from your family and that your kidnapping was staged."

Ferrara's face remained impassive.

"And? Whatever makes you think I owe you an explanation?"

Nate glared at him. "You're the one who dragged me here to pretend to be your boyfriend," he hissed out. "But when Luke just told me that, I had no idea what to say! Now he probably thinks I'm an idiot who has no clue about his own boyfriend's family."

The bastard shrugged. "I see no issue. That's not something I would tell you even if our relationship were real."

"Right. Because you have no idea how relationships work."

Ferrara stepped closer, laid his fingers on Nate's chin, and tipped his face up. Was that amusement in his eyes? "I think you're forgetting something," he said, his voice quiet. "We aren't pretending to be in a serious relationship. We aren't pretending to trust each other. I brought you here to make Demidov think I'm like him. That's all. You aren't my wife. Or husband. No one needs to know my full life story to suck my cock."

Kneel, the word echoed in Nate's mind.

Nate moistened his dry lips with his tongue, his heart beating fast against his ribs and his cock so hard he wanted to scream. "I know. But Luke has gotten it into his head that we're..."

"That we're what?" Ferrara said, his gaze dropping to Nate's mouth for a moment before looking back into Nate's eyes.

Nate felt his face become warm. "That it's a love match," he forced out, feeling painfully awkward.

"A love match," Ferrara repeated, as if the words were in an alien language.

Scoffing, Nate rolled his eyes. "Yes, sometimes people fuck because they love each other. A bizarre concept for you, I know."

"And whatever gave him that idea?"

Nate shot him an incredulous look. "I don't know, maybe the fact that you spent all afternoon yesterday keeping me in your lap and kissing me?"

"Need I remind you that it was your idea?"

"It doesn't matter whose idea it was—that's the impression kissing me for hours gave."

Ferrara's eyes dropped to Nate's lips again.

Nate swallowed, actually feeling his pulse beat rapidly in his neck. Fuck, he hoped he wouldn't have to endure more of those horrible kisses. But they were alone. Ferrara wouldn't kiss him here. He was safe. Totally safe. Nothing was going to happen here. He wouldn't have to endure Ferrara's kisses.

Nate cleared his throat. "So you'd better tell me," he said. "Why did Luke say your kidnapping was staged?"

Sighing, Ferrara looked away and let go of Nate's chin.

Nate hated that he hated the loss of contact.

Ferrara walked to the window and stared out of it, his hands in his pockets, his wide shoulders stiff. "Contrary to popular opinion, my father didn't disown me. He was against me leaving for America and leaving the family business, but he couldn't change my mind once I made the decision. So I left, and he spread the rumor that he kicked me out."

"To protect you?" Nate said.

Ferrara gave a clipped nod. "And himself. He didn't want anyone to use me to get to him. That's why he had to give the impression that he didn't give a shit about me."

"And what, you staged your own kidnapping?"

Ferrara shrugged. "Pretty much. Luke's father, Whitford, was something of an old friend of my father. He agreed to help stage my kidnapping without it being traced back to us."

Nate frowned. "So your kidnapping was fake? It wasn't actually true that you barely survived it?"

A wry smile curled Ferrara's lips.

"By the time I was saved by FBI agents, I really was barely alive. The low-ranking mobsters who were watching over me had no idea that the whole thing was staged, so they weren't exactly gentle."

Nate pursed his lips, wondering. "Was it worth it?"

"Oh, absolutely," Ferrara said, without looking at him. "I don't even need bodyguards these days. In Italy I couldn't take a piss without my bodyguards securing the bathroom first."

Nate thought about it for a moment. "Wait," he said. "Is that why you accepted Demidov's invitation? That's why you were worried, right? Because you knew he was dating Luke Whitford and there was a chance he knew about your staged kidnapping?"

Ferrara gave a nod, stepping closer to him. "I had to find out what he knew—and what he wanted if he really knew that."

That made sense. Except…

"But wasn't it risky for Demidov to invite you to Italy if he suspected that you weren't actually at odds with your family? He could have chosen literally any country but your home country."

Ferrara shook his head. "He knew I wouldn't have accepted the invitation if he invited me somewhere else. The other businessmen invited to the villa were additional assurance that I wasn't walking into a trap. Demidov's willingness to put himself at a disadvantage made it obvious that he wanted something badly enough to want my cooperation. That's why I risked it."

"Luke hinted that Demidov actually wants your help with your father."

Ferrara cocked his head slightly, a twisted smile curling his lips.

"And if I don't cooperate, he'll use me as a bargaining chip against my family now that he has me as his 'guest.'"

Nate opened his mouth to tell him to stop being a cynical asshole, but then stopped, realizing that he didn't actually know Roman Demidov and it was entirely possible. It was entirely possible that the invitation was a setup and they were actually hostages in a fancy cage.

"Shit," he whispered, looking around, suddenly paranoid. "Are we in danger?"

"You? Not really." Ferrara's smile widened. "Unless Demidov gets the brilliant idea that we're a 'love match,' too."

Nate glowered at him, not amused at all. "It's not funny. This could be dangerous! Aren't you afraid at all?"

"Come on, love," Ferrara said gently, his gaze as mock-affectionate as his tone. "Don't you trust me?"

"Ugh, you're such an ass!" Nate said, pushing at Ferrara's chest in frustration.

The asshole caught his fist in a tight grip. "You're forgetting yourself," he said, his voice very soft. "I'm still your boss."

Nate rolled his eyes. "I'll start treating you like my boss when you stop putting your body parts in my mouth." He huffed. "I'm serious, Raffaele. I didn't sign up for this. You may not be scared, but I am, okay?"

The mocking glint was gone from Ferrara's eyes, his expression becoming serious. He held Nate's gaze steadily as he said, "I brought you here. I will not let anything happen to you."

Nate should have laughed. Ferrara couldn't guarantee that at all. But there was something about this man, about his confidence, his arrogance, that was so damn reassuring.

Fuck, he found his horrible boss's arrogance *reassuring*. He needed help, pronto.

"Good," Nate said, trying to shake off the feeling. "Because if I get a bullet in my gut because of you, I'm going to turn into a ghost and haunt you for the rest of your life. Sir."

Ferrara's lips twitched. "That would be dreadful," he said, before closing the distance between them and fitting their mouths together.

Ugh, not this again.

Nate absolutely *detested* the way his brain instantly became fuzzy and disoriented, his world narrowing to Ferrara's hot, domineering mouth that seemed to suck out all of his willpower. He made a feeble attempt to tear his mouth away, but his lips didn't listen to the command from his brain at all, clinging to Ferrara's and parting for his tongue. It was fucking horrible.

He whined when Ferrara finally released his mouth. He glared at him dazedly, rubbing his sensitive lips with the back of his hand. "What was that for?" he hissed. "There's no one here."

The bastard didn't look fazed at all. "Demidov and Whitford will expect you to look well kissed." And then he laid his hand on Nate's nape and steered him back to the breakfast room.

And Nate went.

Chapter 18

As he sat across from Roman Demidov in the man's office, Raffaele felt more annoyed than anything else. He'd left his old life behind for a reason. He didn't enjoy negotiations like this.

He'd always been a good negotiator. He was good at making people bend to his will. It was a quality that made him a good businessman. But these weren't just business negotiations.

The stakes were much higher here.

It had been over a decade since he'd had to deal with men like Demidov—dangerous, unbending, and unpredictable.

It didn't mean he'd forgotten how to.

Raffaele let the silence fall, watching Demidov patiently and keeping his expression neutral. The Russian had the reputation of a ruthless man, but that didn't worry him. He'd been surrounded by men like this since before he could walk. In many ways, their backgrounds were similar, and if it was true that Demidov wanted to leave that part of his life behind, then they really had a lot more in common with each other. But a leopard never changed its spots, even if it wanted to pretend to be a harmless cat. Raffaele didn't delude himself into thinking that this man wasn't dangerous or wouldn't use him for his own gain if he let him.

The silence stretched.

Finally, Demidov sighed, his blue eyes steady on him. "I think it's time we speak candidly," he said.

Raffaele just gave a nod. They had been skirting around the subject for the past few days, conversing only in the presence of others about the business deal Demidov was suggesting—one that had nothing to do with the real reason he was here. It was well past time for them to speak candidly. Raffaele had had the time to evaluate Demidov, and Demidov had likely done the same.

"I want you to convince your father to leave me alone," Demidov finally said, his tone as cold as his gaze. "I have made it clear to him that I'm done doing that sort of business, but he's—dissatisfied and insists that I'm breaking our deal, leaving him without networks in Russia, Eastern Europe, and Central Asia."

"And he can't let it go if he doesn't want to look weak," Raffaele said, suppressing a sigh. Marco's pride had always been one of his greatest flaws.

Demidov nodded, his gaze sharp and assessing. "Frankly, it's something I can handle myself if push comes to shove, but I've been careful to keep my hands clean while I dealt with my other associates, and this is the last one. I'd like to wrap it up without unnecessary… complications. I'm sure you understand what I mean."

Raffaele did, somewhat surprised but careful not to show it. So it was true that Demidov wanted to distance himself from his criminal roots. This issue with the Sicilian Mafia was something that could be resolved by hiring a few talented hitmen, but Demidov was clearly unwilling to risk it, since he wanted to become an upstanding citizen.

Raffaele idly wondered what had motivated this man to do it.

He doubted Demidov had had a sudden change of heart. Men like him generally didn't. Whatever his motives were, they were likely selfish. Just like his own had been.

"I'd like to help you, but my father and I aren't on speaking terms," Raffaele said, meeting Demidov's gaze. "I'm sure you've heard of it."

Demidov's lips twisted into a faint smile. "I've heard of it, yes. And I'm sure you'd like for people to continue hearing that."

"Is that a threat?" Raffaele said, looking at him flatly.

"Not at all," Demidov said, his tone neutral. "I have no interest in threatening you. I want your help, not your unwilling cooperation. Once this… misunderstanding with your father is resolved, I have no intention of blackmailing you. I just want to get it over with."

Raffaele studied him for a moment, looking for any sign of deception.

He found none.

"You will give me whatever evidence you've found among Whitford's possessions," Raffaele said at last. "If you try to double-cross me—"

"I won't," Demidov said, exuding impatience. He opened his desk drawer and pulled out a flash drive. "The originals were deleted, you have my word on it."

Raffaele would have laughed if these were normal business negotiations, but in these circles, where there were rarely any written contracts, a man's word meant a lot, and Roman Demidov didn't have the reputation of someone who didn't keep his word.

He put the flash drive in his pocket and then looked at Demidov. "I will speak to him," he said, getting to his feet. "It might take a few days before I have an answer for you."

"You're welcome to stay here until you get the answer."

Raffaele almost smiled. So for all the supposedly voluntary nature of his help, there clearly was a limit to Demidov's trust. The Russian wanted to keep him close: both to keep an eye on him and to use him as leverage if things went sour with the Sicilian Mafia. They might be "guests," but he wondered what Demidov would do if they attempted to leave.

"We'll stay here," he said, and then paused, somewhat thrown off by the use of "we." It wasn't a word he used often.

Shaking the strange thought off, Raffaele got to his feet and left.

He wasn't entirely happy with how the conversation had gone—or with his own decision. There was a better, more foolproof solution to this issue. All he had to do was tell his family that Demidov knew the truth, and Marco would send his people to take care of the potential risk Demidov presented. It would be a more reliable solution than talking his father into leaving Demidov alone and hoping that the Russian was a man of his word. If anyone else found out that Marco actually gave a damn about his son, Raffaele's comfortable life of an American businessman who didn't need bodyguards would be over. His life would revert to the very existence that he had always loathed: the necessity of bodyguards, random kidnappings, gunfire, and blood. He'd left Italy because he was sick and tired of it. He didn't want to be dragged back into that life.

Demidov was a threat to that. He should have eliminated the threat completely instead of choosing the less reliable route. And for what?

Because you promised Nate you'd keep him safe.

Raffaele ground his teeth, frustrated with himself. But it was true, no matter how much he'd like to deny that. If he told his father to eliminate the threat, the Russian would retaliate. It might get messy very quickly, and the likelihood of Nate being caught in the crossfire was bigger than he'd like.

Fuck, he had gotten soft. Fifteen years ago, he wouldn't have hesitated. But it seemed living in America had changed him, for better or for worse.

Or maybe something else was the culprit.

As if summoned by his thoughts, Nate was right there when he rounded the corner. He was smiling as he talked to some pretty woman—the daughter of a businessman called Nabokov, if Raffaele remembered correctly.

His irritation only spiked at the sight of Nate's wide smile and disgustingly kind expression. That kindness and those nice smiles were never for Raffaele, but they irritated him all the same. He wanted to wipe that smile off Nate's lips. Preferably with his cock. He wanted to stuff it so far down Nate's throat the annoying shit *choked* on it.

His cock twitched in his pants, going full mast, which only served to irritate Raffaele more.

Striding over, he grabbed Nate's nape and yanked him into a bruising kiss. Ignoring the surprised yelp Nate let out against his lips, Raffaele shoved his tongue down his throat, fucking his infuriating mouth the way he wanted to do with his cock. It was the only socially acceptable thing he could do in public. He could hardly open his fly and push Nate to his knees and feed him his cock while the Nabokov chit stood right there.

But fuck, he wanted to.

He kissed Nate harder, keeping his head still in a punishing grip as he plundered his mouth with his tongue. He liked the way his insufferable PA got all confused and submissive whenever Raffaele kissed him. It was heady.

Someone cleared their throat awkwardly, and Raffaele reluctantly broke the kiss. Except Nate didn't let him, his lips clinging to Raffaele's and sucking on his tongue in a way that nearly made him come in his pants like a green boy. Fuck, this was getting out of hand. A mere kiss shouldn't do this to him, regardless of the Ferrara libido. No matter how many times Nate sucked his cock, Raffaele wanted *more*.

Maybe he should just fuck the guy. Push him under him, spread his legs, and take him.

The thought was ridiculously appealing, even though he'd never even entertained fucking another man.

Raffaele broke the kiss, ignoring the whimper Nate let out, and glanced around. The Nabokov chit was gone. He looked back at Nate and studied his flushed face.

"I'm going to fuck you," he stated.

Nate's glassy eyes widened. "Fuck off," he said hoarsely, licking his red, swollen, pretty lips.

Raffaele had to kiss them again.

He felt a rush of vicious satisfaction when Nate immediately opened his mouth for his tongue, his hands clutching at Raffaele's shirt.

When they broke the kiss again to get some air into their lungs, he said against Nate's mouth, "It's going to happen. I always get what I want."

Nate huffed. "Not this time," he said. "Do you even hear yourself? We're both straight."

"So what?" Raffaele said, nipping on his bottom lip. "How is that different from sucking my cock?"

"It's easy for you to say," Nate said with a chuckle, his lips trembling, his hand gripping Raffaele's shirt tightly. "Stop that. Stop kissing me. No one's here."

Raffaele forced his heavy-lidded eyes open and stared at his assistant from a few inches away. Nate's eyes were closed, his cheeks flushed pink and his mouth red and shiny from his kisses.

He wanted to fuck him.

He had to fuck him. He didn't give a shit that Nate was a man too. He wanted to shove Nate under him and *rut* into him, take him like an animal would take a fertile bitch.

"Come on," he said hoarsely, not even recognizing his own voice.

Grabbing Nate's wrist, he pulled him toward their room.

Nate let him.

Chapter 19

Nate had no idea what was going on anymore. His head was spinning, it felt like his mind was filled with cotton, and his limbs felt heavy and not like his own. His traitorous hands were clutching at Ferrara's shoulders, pulling him closer, tighter, his boss's weight heavy on top of him. He could barely breathe, just gasping into Ferrara's mouth and sucking on his tongue.

God, he hated these kisses; he could feel his IQ dropping with every passing minute, all his thoughts focused on how good it felt. He wasn't even sure how he had ended up naked, but the next thing he knew, he was lying naked on their bed under his equally naked boss.

Fuck, he had to stop this. Why were they even doing this? They were straight. No no one was watching them here, so they couldn't even pretend it was for appearances' sake.

"Wait," Nate managed breathlessly as Ferrara sucked bruises into his neck. "I'm serious, I'm not gay."

"Neither am I," Ferrara said with a scoff, his large hands spreading Nate's thighs wide.

Nate flushed, weirded out by the unusual position he was in. His legs were spread wide. As if he were a woman. God, why did the thought make his cock even harder? This was fucked up.

"I don't even like you," Nate tried again. "I loathe you."

"You don't have to like me to have sex with me." Ferrara's hand wrapped around Nate's erection.

Nate nearly came on the spot. Christ, his boss's hand was on his cock. Stroking it. This couldn't possibly be happening.

"I'm not gay, I don't take it up the ass. Sucking your cock is one thing, but this is too much."

A slick finger probed against his asshole. Where had he even gotten lube? Had the bastard planned this? The thought was infuriating.

"Relax."

Nate glared up at him, but he suspected his glare wasn't very effective when they both were naked and his cock was so hard it was already leaking.

"Relax," his boss ordered, his tone harder.

It actually worked—his body had been trained into obeying this man's commands.

The slick finger slipped inside him.

Fuck.

He had his boss's finger in his asshole.

"It feels strange," Nate complained. "I told you I wouldn't like it."

Ferrara gave him a hard look, his black brows furrowed in concentration. "There's supposed to be a—"

Nate jerked as Ferrara crooked his finger, brushing something inside him.

"Your prostate," Ferrara finished, rubbing the same spot.

Nate's mouth fell open in a silent moan, his eyes going wide.

Ferrara looked smug, the asshole.

"Still don't like it?" he said, slipping another finger into him.

"Shut up," Nate hissed, painfully aware of how unconvincing that sounded. Fuck, why did it feel so good? It still felt weird, but good, in a weird way.

Ferrara's lubed fingers were pumping in and out of his hole now, the slick sounds obscene and so damn embarrassing.

Nate had to bite his lips to stop his moans. It felt so intense, this weird need inside of him, building and building, achy and hungry for something. Now the thought of a cock being stuffed into him didn't seem all that unappealing.

"It's just a one-off," Nate said breathlessly, barely keeping his hips still as his boss worked his hole open. "We'll try it once and then we'll never talk about it again. Okay?"

Black eyes swept over his naked body, gleaming with something strange.

"Sure," Raffaele said.

Ferrara, Nate reminded himself stubbornly, but it was hard to make himself think of this man by his last name when he had his goddamn fingers inside of his ass.

"I'm sure I'll hate it anyway," Nate said as the third finger pushed in. His last word became a low groan, it felt so intense—to be stretched like that. His whole world seemed to narrow down to his sensitive hole, stretched wide around those hard fingers. Fuck, he couldn't believe it but his body still craved more.

"Look at you," Raffaele murmured. "You're fucking gagging for it."

Nate glared at him but then he looked down at himself. His face became warmer when he saw his wantonly spread legs and his hard cock standing tall against his abs. Raffaele's fingers looked so dark between his thighs, pumping into his hole in a steady rhythm, the Rolex on his wrist glinting in the muted light.

It looked obscene. He looked obscene.

And it turned him on even more, the utter wrongness of it.

"Just put it in," he bit out, breathing unsteadily as he looked at Raffaele's cock. It looked as mouthwatering as usual, thick and big, the veins on it so prominent Nate wanted to lick them. Lick it. But his hole was clenching around the fingers, wanting more, and the mere idea of that cock inside of him made him ache with need and impatience. He couldn't believe he was actually eager to take it up the ass. To have a man inside of him.

The fingers suddenly pulled out, and he almost whined—he was so damn empty, his hole pulsing around nothing. It was fucking horrible.

He watched hungrily as Raffaele rolled a condom on his cock and then stroked it with his lubed fingers. God, he didn't care how gay it was; he wanted that inside him.

Finally, his boss lined up his cock against Nate's hole, the fat head bumping against it.

"Come on," Nate gritted out, barely stopping himself from pushing back onto the cock like a slut. "Come on, put it in."

Raffaele gripped his thigh harder, his cock teasing his entrance but not actually pushing in.

Panting, Nate glowered at him. "Come on!"

The asshole smiled. "Say the magic word."

"God, I hate you," Nate groaned out, surging forward and kissing him hard, his hand burying in Raffaele's hair. Christ, he wanted to kill this insufferable man, he hated him, he loathed him—he couldn't stop kissing him, his brain turning fuzzy and mushy as soon as

Raffaele's tongue pushed into his mouth. He hooked his legs around Raffaele's hips, feeling like the worst kind of slut but unable to stop. He whined against Raffaele's mouth, and finally—finally—he felt the cock push into him in one hard thrust.

"Ah," Nate cried out, his eyes going wide.

He was so full.

So fucking full.

The cock in him felt so thick and big it brushed against his prostate without even trying, pressing against it, the sensation so intense he nearly passed out. He wanted more of this. It was the best and the worst feeling in the world, because he knew with sudden clarity that he wouldn't be able to live without this, would crave this feeling always. "More," he growled, gyrating his hips and trying to make the other man move.

Raffaele made a strange, guttural noise and started moving. Fucking. Pistoning in and out of him with hard thrusts that made the mattress shake. It was exactly what Nate needed. What he wanted.

He moaned, loud and shameless, his fingers digging into Raffaele's muscular buttocks, trying to pull him deeper into him. God…

They fucked like animals in mating season, the bed creaking under them so loudly it was probably audible in the corridor. Nate couldn't care less. He just wanted, shaking with the weird need inside him, the kind he'd never felt before.

A small, distant part of him couldn't believe that this shameless creature coming apart on another man's cock was him. But it was him. He was this guy who had his legs wantonly spread for another man, moaning non-stop. God, so good, it felt so good…

Raffaele wrapped his hand around his aching cock and *squeezed*.

Nate's orgasm slammed into him. He moaned, and Raffaele swallowed his moan, his tongue plunging inside of his mouth with every thrust of his hips, fucking Nate's blissed-out body through his orgasm.

God.

Jesus fucking Christ.

So good.

Vaguely, he was aware of the man on top of him still thrusting, using him to chase his own orgasm, but he couldn't bring himself to mind, still lost to pleasure.

Raffaele buried his face into his neck, groaned, and finally went still, shuddering as he spilled into the condom. Nate had the bizarre thought that he would have liked to know what it felt like to have him come inside him.

The thought made his spent cock twitch.

For a long moment, there was only silence as they panted together, sweaty and spent, Raffaele's bulk on top of him heavy but not uncomfortably so, their heads on the same pillow.

Nate breathed deeply, inhaling the scent of sex, man, and aftershave, and waited for the inevitable freak out to come.

But so far, it had failed to materialize. He felt fucked out and mellow in the best sense of the word. He felt so damn wonderful—the best he'd ever felt in his life, actually.

"Well, that was a bust," Nate said with a sigh. "I didn't hate it."

That was the understatement of the century. He already felt embarrassingly eager for more, acutely aware of the cock still buried inside him.

Raffaele exhaled loudly and didn't say anything, just watching Nate with his dark eyes, only a scant few inches separating their faces.

As always, his boss's intensity made him feel strange, but Nate knew he'd feel even weirder when Raffaele shifted his gaze to something else.

Yeah, apparently he could still get so flustered over a simple look when he had the man's cock still buried inside of him.

He clenched his ass around said cock and nearly moaned when he felt it start hardening again.
Satan's insane libido was finally good for something.

"Stop that," Raffaele bit off and moved to pull out, but Nate whined in protest, wrapping his legs around his hips.

"Just one more time," he said before he could stop himself. He flushed, unable to believe his own behavior—he really was acting like a cock slut.

Raffaele eyed him for a moment, his gaze so very dark and intense. "All right," he said and moved his hips. "Just one more time."

Nate pulled him down into a greedy kiss.

Chapter 20

The "one more time" mantra turned out to be a running theme for the next week. It was absolutely horrible, but Nate couldn't stop. It was a good thing the majority of the guests had already left the villa, because he couldn't seem to keep it in his pants even when they were outside the bedroom.

They fucked in the pool, with Nate gripping the edge of it as Raffaele fucked him from behind. They fucked in a lounge chair on the beach, without even bothering with lube because Nate was still slick and sloppy after morning sex and couldn't wait to get fucked. They fucked in the library, fully clothed but for Nate's shorts on the floor, his legs spread wide as he clutched at Raffaele's shirt and bit his own lips to stop himself from moaning. He felt like the worst kind of cock slut, but he couldn't get enough, insatiable.

One look into his boss's dark eyes and he was half-hard, his hands tingling with the urge to reach down and pull out Raffaele's cock, which seemed to be always up for it. Fuck, he felt like a goddamn nympho. Or maybe Raffaele's ridiculous libido was just catching. Either way, he couldn't seem to stop spreading his legs for his asshole of a boss every chance he got.

Case in point: they were having dinner with Luke and Demidov, but Nate couldn't really focus on the food, no matter how delicious it looked and tasted.

His eyes kept straying to Raffaele, who was talking to Luke about soccer, of all things.

Nate tried not to stare at him blatantly, but he probably failed. His eyes trailed over the powerful muscles straining Raffaele's black shirt, and he licked his lips, remembering how good they felt to the touch, how good they looked as they flexed when Raffaele fucked into him.

Stop that, he told himself, beyond annoyed. He could live a few hours without being fucked or thinking about being fucked. It was the first time in days that they'd bothered socializing with their hosts. Nate knew there was a reason for that—he was pretty sure Raffaele had mentioned something about a phone call he'd finally received, but it all was pretty hazy, to be honest, because they had been in the middle of sex and Nate hadn't really given a fuck about anything but Raffaele's mouth against his lips and his cock inside him.

Luke laughed at something Raffaele said and shook his head. "Chelsea is totally winning the Champions' League this year, I'm sure of it. DuVal is too good. I'm sure he'll win the Golden Boot, too."

"He's past his prime as a player," Raffaele said, his eyes trained on Luke.

It suddenly occurred to Nate that Luke was very pretty. He was prettier than most women.

Nate's jaw tightened in annoyance. *So what?* he snapped at himself. It didn't matter that Nate looked like a plain oaf compared to a twink like Luke. He was a normal guy. He didn't want to look *pretty*, for fuck's sake. He didn't give a shit if Raffaele wanted to fuck Luke. He didn't.

Irritated with himself, Nate ripped his gaze away from the pair and looked at Demidov.

The Russian seemed content enough to sip his tea and watch his lover's animated conversation with another man. There wasn't a hint of jealousy or insecurity in his eyes.

Roman Demidov was a handsome man, objectively. His skin was kind of too pale for Nate's liking, but the combination of his dark hair and blue eyes was striking. He clearly was in great shape, too.

Nate tried to imagine having sex with him. Tried to imagine allowing him to fuck him. The idea... wasn't completely repulsive, but it was definitely very weird. He just couldn't imagine it. Couldn't imagine being into it.

"Let's go for a walk," Raffaele suddenly said, gripping his wrist and dragging him to his feet.

Startled, Nate allowed it and followed him in silence until they walked a significant distance away from the beach patio.

"He's not interested in fucking you."

It took Nate's brain a few moments to catch up. He glared at Raffaele, yanking his wrist from his grip. "Fuck off. I didn't say I wanted to fuck him."

Raffaele's lips twisted into something derisive. "It was written all over your face, with the way you were studying him like a piece of meat."

Nate's fingers itched to wipe that sneer away with his fist. Or with his mouth—and that infuriated him even more. "I'm surprised you even noticed with the way you were chatting up Luke."

Those black eyebrows raised. "If I didn't know better, I'd think you were jealous."

God, he hated him.

"In your dreams," Nate ground out through his gritted teeth. "I simply don't want Demidov to take offense just because you suddenly decided that you like fucking men."

"You think I like fucking men?" Raffaele said, stopping and turning to him. There was an expression of genuine surprise on his face.

Nate scoffed, crossing his arms over his chest. "You seemed to like it plenty this morning. And this afternoon. And yesterday four times."

The insufferable man had the nerve to laugh, his white teeth flashing against his sun-bronzed skin.

"What?" Nate snapped. "What's so funny? Are you going to claim you actually don't like it?"

Raffaele put his hand on Nate's nape and pulled him closer.

Nate wet his lips with his tongue, hating the way his heartbeat picked up and his lips were tingling in anticipation of a kiss already. Fuck, he needed help. Why did he feel like a junkie who was about to be given his drug?

"I don't like fucking men," Raffaele said, almost against his mouth.

His eyelids growing heavy, Nate parted his lips. *Please.*

Raffaele nipped on Nate's bottom lip. "It just turns me on to see how much you love having my cock in you."

"I don't," Nate said and whimpered when Raffaele pushed his tongue into his mouth. He sucked on it with relish, heat spreading to his lower stomach, to his cock and balls.

"You do," Raffaele said when he allowed him to breathe. "I've never seen a cock slut like you. If you were a woman, you'd be wet for me all the time."

Nate shivered. "Fuck you," he said weakly.

Raffaele's hand slid down his back and then slipped under the waistband of Nate's shorts. A finger stroked right over Nate's hole.

Nate gasped, his hole twitching.

"See? You're fucking wet."

Nate flushed. "It's lube, you ass."

"Exactly," Raffaele said, biting his earlobe. "You haven't even bothered to clean yourself down there. You actually *like* feeling loose and sloppy, don't you?"

Nate didn't say anything. Couldn't. All his efforts were on not making any sound as Raffaele's finger massaged his hole in circular motions. God. God.

"Look at you," Raffaele said hoarsely. "You're letting me finger you in public, on a beach where anyone can see us."

Nate buried his face in Raffaele's shoulder to muffle his moan.

"Roman and Luke can probably still see us," Raffaele said in a low voice, pushing the finger in. "Do you think they can see where my hand is?"

"God, shut up," Nate moaned, pushing back against that finger. Fuck it, maybe he was a slut.

Raffaele slipped a second finger into him and started scissoring them. "I'm surprised you thought you were straight considering how much you love taking it up the ass."

"Fuck you," Nate bit out, his eyes rolling to the back of his head.

Christ, he'd never get enough of this feeling.

"In a moment," Raffaele said. He steered Nate slightly without withdrawing his fingers and then sat down on a big rock, pulling Nate into his lap. It took only a moment to kick Nate's shorts off.

Nate was the one to unzip his boss's slacks and pull out his hard cock. He gave it a reverent, greedy stroke, before pulling a condom out of Raffaele's pocket and rolling it on in one smooth motion. He'd had lots of practice by now.

As soon as Raffaele withdrew his fingers, Nate shifted and pushed himself down on the hard length. He panted, his mouth opening and closing as he took all of that cock inside. God, it was the best fucking feeling in the world.

"As I said, a cock slut," Raffaele said softly, nipping along his jaw. "Anyone can come across us. See those boats? They are probably full of tourists with binoculars. They can probably see you bouncing eagerly on my cock."

Nate moaned, riding him harder, the mere idea only turning him on more. "I hate you," he said before crushing their mouths together.

It didn't take him long to come, groaning and shaking with his whole body. He sagged against Raffaele's broad shoulder, gasping and trying to catch his breath as Raffaele rocked up into him, chasing his own orgasm.

He was still basking in the afterglow when he had an inane thought.

He never wanted to leave this villa.

He never wanted this to end.

Chapter 21

But as all things, their stay in Italy came to an end.

That night, as they lay in the bed, exhausted and sated after their last round of sex, Raffaele broke the companionable silence. "I've booked our tickets back. The plane leaves tomorrow morning."

Nate opened his eyes and digested that for a few moments, his damp cheek pressed against Raffaele's chest. He kind of felt gross and sticky, but he felt too lazy to get up and take a shower. To his surprise, Raffaele wasn't pushing him away. It was a little weird. Nate knew how sensitive his boss was to smells, and yet... Raffaele seemed perfectly content to put up with Nate's sweaty body sprawled on top of him.

"I didn't know you knew how to book tickets," Nate said at last. "Isn't that your assistant's job?"

"I'm capable of booking a few tickets," Raffaele said, very dryly.

"So the trip was a success?" Nate said, his fingers playing with the black hairs on Raffaele's leg.

"We did strike a deal beneficial for the Caldwell Group."

Nate smacked him on the thigh. "Don't play dumb. You know what I mean."

"The trip was a success on both counts," Raffaele said, sighing. "My father agreed to leave Demidov alone... after some concessions from the Russian."

Nate didn't even want to know. It would probably be better if he didn't ask, actually.

"I guess it wasn't for nothing, then."

Raffaele threaded his fingers through Nate's hair in an absentminded manner and just hummed, sounding half-asleep already.

Nate absolutely detested how much he loved this, how much he loved being curled up against Raffaele's firm body and just... existing beside him. This intimate, companionable air between them scared him much more than the way he was hopelessly addicted to the sex. Sex was just sex. This feeling of blissed-out contentment was far more dangerous.

What were they doing?

What was this?

His anxiety rising, Nate chewed on his lip, looking at the other man. Raffaele had his eyes closed, his breathing steady. But Nate knew he wasn't actually asleep yet.

"I can practically hear you think," Raffaele said, without opening his eyes.

"What's going to happen when we get back?" Nate said, propping himself on his elbow.

Dark eyelashes fluttered open. Black eyes stared at him with an inscrutable expression. "Try to be a little more specific."

Nate pursed his lips, frustrated that he even had to explain this. "What happens in Italy, stays in Italy and all that?" He hadn't meant to make it sound like a question. It wasn't a question. It couldn't be a question.

Raffaele's face was unreadable.

After a moment, he said, "It's probably for the best. You're already cuddly and needy. I don't want you to get ideas that this is a relationship."

Nate flushed, pulling away as if burned. Cuddly? *Needy*? "Fuck you—I'm not an idiot."

"Hm," Raffaele said, closing his eyes again.

Nate glared at him, so damn annoyed he didn't know what to do with it. "God, you're such an ass! I hate everything about you. I wouldn't want a relationship with you even if you were the last person on Earth!"

A muscle jumped in Raffaele's cheek. "I'm glad to hear that," he said, without opening his eyes. "Be quiet now. We have an early flight tomorrow."

Scowling, Nate turned the bedside lamp off and lay down as far from his dick of a boss as it was possible to do.

Neither of them said goodnight.

***

Nate was kind of surprised Luke and Demidov had bothered to get up so early to see them off. Luke was still yawning, and there was a pillow crease on Demidov's face that gave him a more approachable look. He looked like a normal human being for once.

"Thanks for your help," Luke said, shaking Raffaele's hand. "We really appreciate it."

Raffaele just nodded and laid his hand on Nate's nape. "Into the car," he commanded, clearly wanting to exchange a few words with Demidov without him present.

Keeping his face blank, Nate waved awkwardly at Luke and strode toward the car. The bodyguards were putting their baggage into it. He muttered, "Good morning" and received a laconic "*Buongiorno*" in response. It was still more conversation than he'd gotten from Raf—Ferrara this morning. Ferrara. He had to go back to thinking of him as Ferrara. His boss. And nothing else.

He got into the car and watched Ferrara shake Demidov's hand. Then Ferrara was heading to the car, his expression somewhat thoughtful. Nate dragged his gaze away and looked back at the couple. Luke waved, smiling at him and mouthing "Text me," his curly head on Demidov's shoulder. The Russian wrapped his arm around his lover's waist and held him close.

Nate felt a pang of wistfulness. Or maybe envy. He wanted to find someone who would look at him the way Demidov looked at Luke—as if he were the most important thing in the world. He wondered if they'd get married. Probably.

Ferrara opened the door and got into the car, and Nate's whole focus snapped back to him.

Pursing his lips, he pulled his phone out and fixed his gaze on it, as if every cell of his body wasn't hyperaware of the man beside him.

"Milano," Ferrara told the driver, without even glancing at him.

Nate sighed inwardly.

It was going to be a long flight.

***

Thirteen hours later, Nate finally crawled into his bed, nearly groaning from how amazing it felt. Even a first class seat was nowhere near as comfy as his own bed. The angry tension between him and his boss hadn't exactly helped him relax, either.

"You're finally back!" Maya said, plopping down on his bed next to him. "How was Italy?"

"I posted pics on my Instagram," Nate grumbled.

"Just on the first day, and then nothing."

Yeah, because I was too busy sucking my boss's face and spreading my legs for him, Nate thought glumly.

"Okay, what happened? I know you. Spill."

Nate sighed, but there was no point in trying to hide it. His sister knew him too well. "I had sex with him."

The resulting silence was deafening.

"You did what?" Maya half-shouted, half-shrilled. "Like, buttsex?"

Nate buried his face deeper into his pillow, his skin burning with embarrassment. "Yes."

"Did you like it?" Maya sounded curious. "Getting fucked? Was it weird?"

"Why do you assume I was the one who took it up the ass? Maybe I fucked him."

Maya laughed. "Sorry, but from everything you told me about him, he sounds like such a top. Though maybe he's versatile. Is he?"

"No," Nate grumbled. He was annoyed that the idea of fucking Raffaele hadn't even occurred to him—he just hadn't wanted that, too addicted to getting fucked.

"He didn't force you, right?" Maya said, her voice losing all humor.

Nate nearly laughed, wondering what she would say if she knew how eager Nate had been to get a dick into him. "He didn't. I told you he's not like that."

"So did you like it?" she pressed.

He groaned, knowing that she wouldn't leave him alone until he told her. "It was fine."

"Fine? Come on, you can do better than that."

"What do you want me to say?" Nate snapped, his pent-up frustration finally bursting out. "That I loved it? I loved it so much that we fucked all the time while we were there?"

Maya was quiet for a while.

Nate was glad he couldn't see her face. Christ, this was so mortifying.

"It's nothing to be ashamed of, dumbass," she said at last.

"Easy for you to say."

"I don't really see a problem," she said. "So you like fucking guys. Big deal. I'm sure Mom and Dad won't care if you tell them you're bi."

Nate opened his mouth and closed it, unable to say it. How could he tell his sister that he wasn't even sure that he was bi? That he couldn't imagine allowing some other guy to fuck him in the ass—being eager for it? The mere idea just seemed... strange. Wrong.

He tried not to think about what it meant.

"It doesn't matter," Nate muttered. "We decided that what happened in Italy stays in Italy." Raffaele Ferrara was just his boss. Nate was his personal assistant. Nothing more. Nate would go back to running errands for him, while Raffaele would go back to fucking his booty calls.

His stomach tied up into a knot, and Nate bit the inside of his cheek, hard.

It was fine. Totally fine.

He could do it.

He wasn't *needy*, thank you very much.

Chapter 22

There was something maddening about your boss standing there over you when you were trying to focus on your damn job.

Nate glared at the monitor in front of him, putting all his focus on typing instead of the man who stood behind him, dictating—Nate actually had no idea what he was dictating. He typed the words, but they didn't seem to make any sense, his body painfully aware of the other man. He even had to breathe shallower in order not to get a whiff of Ra—*Ferrara's* scent.

"This here is wrong," Ferrara said, laying a hand on Nate's shoulder and leaning over to point at something on the screen.

Inhaling shakily, Nate nodded, seeing nothing, his head empty of all thought.

He wanted to grab the asshole by the tie and—

Focus.

If he didn't know better, he'd think the bastard was being all over his personal space on purpose, trying to drive him crazy.

But that made no sense. Raffaele was the one who had said that Nate was being disgustingly *needy* and cuddly. It would make no fucking sense for him to enable that behavior. Right?

"Nate, are you going to lunch with us—Oh. Good morning, sir. I mean, good afternoon, Mr. Ferrara."

Nate exhaled in relief when Raffaele pulled away from him and straightened up.

Nate smiled shakily at Sasha, a cheerful girl from the marketing department, and got to his feet. "Sure," he said, putting his computer to sleep. His hands didn't shake. Much. "I'll finish this after lunch, sir," he said quickly, without looking at Raffaele, and strode toward Sasha, who was waiting for him by the elevator.

"Holy crap, did you see the look on his face?" Sasha whispered quietly, taking his arm. "I nearly pissed myself. How can you put up with him all the time? You should be given a medal!"

Nate pressed his lips together. "He's not that bad," he said, and then immediately wanted to smack himself.

He's not that bad? Really?

From the look on Sasha's face, she clearly thought he was nuts.

Just great.

Nate resolved to do better, but try as he might, he couldn't seem to quash the urge to defend Raffaele to his co-workers as they shared lunch. The worst part was, it genuinely bothered him when his friends bad-mouthed him. It had never bothered him before. But now he couldn't seem to shut up whenever one of his friends said something cutting about Raffaele.

"How is that fucking fair that Linden was fired just because he said he wouldn't work overtime?" Ron said, to a chorus of agreement from his co-workers. "He's an asshole."

Nate bit his tongue, trying to stop himself from speaking again, but it was useless. "Linden wasn't fired for refusing to work overtime," he said, fixing his gaze on his mug of coffee.

"He was fired for going to that journalist and spreading false information that the overtime is forced and unpaid. You know it isn't true." Those nasty rumors spread like wildfire, causing hundreds of clickbait articles that made people "cancel" the company. Nate had his issues with the Caldwell Group's corporate policies and crunch, but that time the backlash was uncalled for.

"Well, yeah," Ron said, deflating a little. "But it's not like we can really refuse to crunch—being paid triple is too good an offer to turn down. Only an idiot would turn it down."

Nate nearly snapped, *If you're too greedy to turn it down, don't blame it on him.*

But he held the scathing remark back. Barely.

By the time the lunch was over, Nate felt pain in his knuckles from how hard he had been clenching his fists, and he was incredibly annoyed with himself for feeling so damn protective of a man who didn't deserve it. Raffaele wasn't a good man. His co-workers' complaints and grievances were partly justified. Partly. Because they weren't really being fair to him. Raffaele wasn't a hypocrite. They didn't know how much he worked. They didn't know that Raffaele was one of the last people to leave the building every day—and *he* actually wasn't paid for that. They didn't know him. They didn't know him like Nate did.

"For fuck's sake," Nate muttered under his breath, heading back to the office.

Stop. Just stop.

***

"What happens in Italy, stays in Italy" was a good idea. In theory.

In practice, Nate just couldn't look at Raffaele—*Ferrara*, dammit—with the same eyes. Not when he knew exactly how his boss looked under his designer suits. Not when he knew what it felt like to sleep curled up next to him, with his hand on his bare chest, feeling his strong, steady heartbeat. Not when he knew what that mouth and that stubble felt like against his face, his mouth, his belly, his inner thigh, his—

Nate ripped his gaze away and tried to focus it on the project leader reporting on his progress.

Job. He must focus on the job. Raffaele was his boss. Nothing more.

But a few moments later, his gaze was drawn back to Raffaele, as though by a magnet.

He stared at Raffaele's strong fingers playing with his pen absentmindedly while Raffaele listened to the report, and licked his suddenly dry lips as he remembered those very fingers pushing into him, fingering his hole loose, preparing it for his cock.

Nate's cock went from half-hard to painfully hard in an instant. He bit the inside of his cheek, hating himself a little, but it seemed his stupid body hadn't gotten the memo that it wouldn't be getting this man on top of him and inside of him ever again.

At that moment, Raffaele looked right at him.

Their gazes locked, and held.

And held.

Nate's pulse was hammering against his throat. He hoped he didn't look as thirsty as he felt.

At long last, his boss shifted his eyes back to the project leader, and Nate exhaled, feeling relieved… and terribly disappointed. God, this was fucked-up.

The meeting seemed to crawl.

By the time it finally ended, Nate felt like punching someone. Or screaming. Or crawling into his boss's lap and kissing him right there, everything and everyone be damned. It was *unbearable.*

He was still struggling to compose himself when he followed Raffaele into his office.

The door clicked shut.

Nate stared numbly as Raffaele shrugged out of his dark suit and loosened his dark-red tie.

"Shirt," he said in a clipped voice without looking at Nate.

Right.

Raffaele wanted to change his shirt. It was nothing out of the ordinary.

Nate turned and went to the closet. Opened it. The row of pristine shirts stared back at him.

Grabbing a blue one, he turned and walked to his boss on legs that felt like rubber, his heart thundering like crazy.

He watched those tan fingers unbutton the white shirt, revealing the smooth, muscular chest with a trail of dark hair disappearing into the waistband of Raffaele's suit pants. His mouth was so dry he had to lick his lips twice. Until Raffaele, Nate had never looked at a man's body and thought *hot*. But now he couldn't look at Raffaele's strong shoulders and arms without feeling thirsty as fuck. Even the veins on Raffaele's forearms were somehow sexy.

He wanted to lick them.

Raffaele dropped the shirt to the floor. Normally Nate would berate him for that. But he said nothing this time, trying to fight the wave of dizzying arousal as he gazed at his boss's muscular, sun-bronzed torso, his fingers itching to touch those pecs, those brown nipples, that hard stomach and then…

Nate swallowed and looked up into Raffaele's black eyes.

The moment stretched.

He had no idea who moved first, but suddenly they were kissing, so hard it almost hurt. God. Nate's mind went absolutely blank with overwhelming *want*. He sucked on Raffaele's tongue, his hands clutching his bare back helplessly. He was whining, trying to pull him closer, so close there wasn't any space between them. Fuck, it felt so good, but he was so hungry for this—for him—after days of not touching him that it wasn't enough. He unbuckled Raffaele's belt with impatient, shaky fingers, and yanked his zipper open.

After that… Nate wasn't sure what happened after that. There was just Raffaele's hot mouth, the taste of him, the feel of his firm body against his, his hands—those amazing hands—wrapping around both of their hard cocks as Raffaele rutted against him on his desk. Nate was gasping and moaning, wanting *more*, more of this man on top of him, inside of him, all the time. He knew he was too loud; it was lucky the room was well insulated.

He came so fast it would have been embarrassing if he didn't feel Raffaele come a second later, shuddering and spilling against Nate's thigh.

They breathed together shakily, panting and coming down from the high, hands still clutching at each other. God, so good. He never wanted to let go.

When Nate's brain started functioning again, he sighed. So much for *what happens in Italy, stays in Italy*. He'd just come, but he already wanted more.

"You turned me into a goddamn nympho," Nate complained.

A laugh left Raffaele's mouth.

Blinking, Nate pulled back a little and looked at him. He'd rarely heard him laugh like that, without any sardonic undertone. It made him look so much younger.

"I don't think that's possible," Raffaele said, smiling wryly.

Nate almost smiled back. "You did. You turned me from a normal guy into this… this…"

"Cock slut?"

Nate flushed. "I was going to say an insatiable, sex-obsessed thing, but that works, too."

A corner of Raffaele's mouth twitched again.

"It's not funny!" Nate said, threading his fingers through Raffaele's hair. He couldn't stop touching him. "This is horrible."

"It's just sex," Raffaele said with a shrug. "I'm sure if we fuck often enough, we'll tire of it. I always do."

Nate pursed his lips. But it made some sense. If this wasn't just going away, fucking until it got boring might be a solution.

"You said you didn't want me to get any ideas that it's a relationship," Nate reminded him. The memory made him scowl.

Raffaele's expression changed somewhat, but it was difficult to read. "Then don't get ideas. Simple."

Considering the disastrous lunch with his co-workers and his weird protectiveness, Nate wasn't sure it was that simple.

"You're my boss," he tried again. "I don't even like you."

"Good," Raffaele said before biting Nate's bottom lip. "I don't want you to like me and ruin everything. This is perfectly good."

Right. It made sense. Probably. Nate wasn't sure; his mind quickly became clouded again. Fuck, Raffaele's *mouth*. All he wanted was more.

"Do you have lube here?" he mumbled against Raffaele's lips, burying his fingers in his hair and deepening the kiss greedily. Dry-humping wasn't enough for him. He wanted to be fucked. He missed being fucked several times a day, completely hooked on the feeling. He wanted this man inside of him, all the time—until he got bored of it.

It had to happen eventually.

It had to.

Chapter 23

Three months later

Nate moaned, his glazed eyes fixed on the ceiling of the office unseeingly as Raffaele pounded into him. God, nothing should feel this fucking good. He couldn't get enough of this. It felt like he was born to take that cock and every minute that it wasn't inside him felt like a waste. If sex addiction was a thing, Nate definitely had it. To his growing desperation, he wasn't getting tired of it at all. If anything, it had become worse: now even Raffaele's scent turned him on—hell, everything about him turned him on. Nate had to actively stop himself from kissing him at random moments in front of other people.

"Want you deeper," he muttered deliriously, trying to pull him closer, *tighter*. Unlike Nate, Raffaele was fully clothed but for his open fly, and the contrast between them only turned him on more.

Raffaele pulled out and slammed hard into him. Nate cried out.

"Look at you," Raffaele said, his glazed black eyes roaming over Nate's naked body. "You're so desperate for cock. Would any cock do? Or do you want just mine?"

Part of him, the distant part that was still able to think, noted the strangeness of the question, the possessiveness of it.

But people said weird shit during sex. He shouldn't overthink it. "Yours," Nate mumbled, pulling Raffaele down into a needy kiss. God, he wanted to consume him, swallow him whole. "Want you. So much."

Raffaele groaned and started fucking him harder, his thrusts losing rhythm and becoming erratic until he shuddered and spilled into the condom. It felt amazing, to feel him lose control and come before him—something that almost never happened. It was so damn hot, but it left Nate unsatisfied. He whined in frustration, clenching around the softening cock in him.

Raffaele kissed his neck before dropping to his knees in front of him. He pushed Nate's spread legs even wider and then—

Nate wailed, his eyes rolling to the back of his head as Raffaele took his hard cock into his mouth. It was the hottest fucking thing he'd ever seen—to see his proud, domineering boss on his knees, sucking his cock. But it still wasn't enough. His hole was throbbing, aching to be filled, and Nate whined in frustration.

"I know what you want," Raffaele said, pulling off his cock and moving his head lower. He licked his hole, and Nate moaned, delirious.

"You don't want your cock sucked," Raffaele said between licks. "You want me to eat you out, lick your greedy little hole."

"Shut up," Nate said weakly, his face burning. "I hate dirty talk."

"Liar," Raffaele said, sucking on his hole, before licking it, again and again. "You're a slut for it."

"Shut up and eat me out," Nate said, burying his fingers in Raffaele's hair and pressing his face tighter against his ass. *More.*

Raffaele chuckled and pushed his tongue inside him. Nate came so hard he nearly blacked out.

***

Really, it was a wonder they got any work done.

By the time Nate got home that day, he'd been fucked three times. His ass felt a little sore when he moved, but after months of this, his body was used to it and didn't complain much. Nate was aware that it was probably kind of messed-up that he *liked* feeling the soreness. It reminded him of Raffaele even when he wasn't there.

"Are we going to finally talk about it?"

Nate came to a stop and winced. "Hey. I'm tired. Can we talk tomorrow—"

"No, we can't," Maya said from the couch, where she had apparently been lying in wait for him. "It's ten in the evening, Nate. Ten! This is ridiculous!"

"We had lots of work," Nate said defensively. "I'm being paid for overtime."

"Lots of work," Maya said, practically radiating skepticism. She got to her feet and walked over. She sniffed. "Is that why you smell of some cologne? It's a very nice cologne, I'll give you that."

"It's new," Nate said. "Do you like it?"

Maya gave him a flat look. "You don't wear cologne. Even if you did, you wouldn't be able to afford such an expensive one."

"Wow, you can tell the price by the scent alone?" Nate said with a weak chuckle.

His sister smacked him on the head. "Stop playing dumb. You think I'm stupid? You think I don't know what's going on just because you're barely home? I'm going to ask you one question. And you're going to answer me honestly. Why are you still sleeping with your asshole of a boss, you dunderhead?"

Nate swallowed.

He didn't have an answer. He honestly didn't know how to answer—how to justify his irresponsible behavior.

And he knew it was irresponsible.

They had been ridiculously lucky that no one had come across them so far and the gossip hadn't spread through the entire building. No one would ever take him seriously as a game designer if it became known that he was the boss's fucktoy. His career would be ruined before it even properly started. Even if he managed to get employed by another company in a different city even, the rumors would follow him everywhere. The video gaming industry was very close-knit, with people changing studios very often, so the rumors about his misconduct would be everywhere.

He might as well move to Siberia.

"I…" He bit his lip, unable to meet his sister's eyes. "I just… I can't stop. I can't, okay?"

She sighed. "You're an idiot. It can only end very badly for you, you know that, right?"

Nate smiled humorlessly. "Yeah. I know." Either Raffaele would get tired of him or they would get caught. He couldn't think of any other outcome.

He had accepted by now that he wasn't getting tired of Raffaele.

"Is he that good?"

Nate shrugged, looking anywhere but at his sister. "I just can't think when he's close. But I can't stand not having him close, either."

He could feel Maya's troubled look with his skin.

"You know what?" she said at last. "Go get changed. We're going out tonight. You will pick up a pretty girl—or a handsome guy. Have sex with someone other than him."

Running a hand through his hair, Nate pulled a face. "I'm tired, Maya. I'm not really in the mood."

She snorted. "You're never tired for *him*. Stop whining and get dressed. Wear something good. We're going out."

"Come on, I have to go to work early tomorrow—"

"You're young and healthy. You can function one day on four hours of sleep. Now get dressed. Or I'll start thinking you have feelings for that asshole."

That shut Nate up. Because—nope, he wasn't going there. Just no.

It took him fifteen minutes to take a quick shower and get dressed in something decent. He yawned, studying himself in the mirror. He looked all right, but tired. He really was tired and not in the mood to get laid by some random person. The mere thought turned his stomach—because he didn't like one-night stands. It had nothing to do with Raffaele, no matter what Maya might have implied.

"You ready?" Maya said.

Nate nodded with forced enthusiasm.

The club was just like any other club out there.

Nate suppressed a wince at the noise, the loud music causing a dull headache at the top of his forehead. All he wanted was sleep. Hooking up with someone was the last thing he wanted. But Maya was like a bulldog with a bone. She wouldn't have let it go if he had just refused to go. She would have drawn all kinds of conclusions—the wrong conclusions.

"Smile," Maya said. "Go get us drinks. Talk to people. Flirt. Live a little, come on!"

Sighing, Nate did as he was told. He went to the bar and ordered them drinks. He settled against the bar and people-watched. People sometimes came over and tried to pick him up. Women and men alike. The latter surprised him a little. Did he give off that vibe now?

The thought made him... not upset, exactly, but a little uneasy. Had he changed that fundamentally that people could tell just by looking at him?

"It's pretty hot in here, right?" the guy—Arnold or something—said, trying to shout over the loud music. He was older and fairly attractive. "How about getting some fresh air at the back?" His flirtatious smile strongly hinted that he wanted to get more than just "fresh air."

Nate gripped his drink harder. "I'm good, thanks," he said, before gulping it down.

The alcohol hit his system hard and fast, so fast that he felt nearly dizzy for a moment. Right. He hadn't eaten anything since lunch and he was tired; of course the booze would affect him much faster than normal.

The guy said something again, but Nate could barely hear it over the music.

"What?" he yelled.

Arnold leaned right to his ear and said, his breath tickling Nate's ear, "I really want to suck your cock."

Nate blinked a few times, his alcohol-addled brain struggling to keep up.

"Or you can suck mine," the guy said with a leer, looking at his lips.

Nate felt nausea rise in his throat. He shook his head, dazed and confused. "No," he said. Why was everything spinning? The alcohol shouldn't have affected him so strongly, no matter how hungry and tired he was. Had his drink been spiked?

His anxiety rising, Nate tried to search the crowd for his sister, but he couldn't find her in the sea of dancing people.

"You shouldn't have done it," he managed—slurred out, barely able to focus his gaze on the guy.

"Done what?" Arnold said innocently, his hand creeping up Nate's thigh and stroking his half-hard cock. Nausea and arousal hit Nate at once in equal measure. He couldn't move. He couldn't do anything. It felt like his limbs weighed a ton.

"You don't want to do this," Nate heard himself slur out. "I'm not here alone."

Arnold glanced around. "I've been watching you. I haven't seen you with anyone."

Fuck, where was Maya when he needed her?

"Then you're an idiot," Nate said, finally forcing his limbs to move. "Fuck off, dude." He staggered away from the bar, his unfocused gaze trying and failing to find his sister. He could feel Arnold following him but not attempting to touch him, probably waiting for the right opportunity. Nate considered his options, but there weren't many. Maya had the car keys and he couldn't drive in this state anyway. He could try to call his sister, but she was unlikely to hear him over the loud music. He needed to find a quieter place. A quieter, safer place.

He staggered into the men's room, and to his relief, there were two guys there, pissing at the urinals. Arnold followed him inside but couldn't grab him without attracting unwanted attention.

Nate got into the nearest bathroom stall and locked the door with shaking fingers, his cock uncomfortably hard.

Then he pushed the toilet lid down and sank onto the seat. Finding his sister's number, he pressed Call.

The door rattled.

Gripping his phone harder, Nate waited, silently begging Maya to pick up. She would never let him live it down if she had to save him from some creep, but he had no other options. Calling anyone else would be so damn humiliating. He was a grown man. He shouldn't need rescuing.

"I'm calling the police," Nate said loudly. "So fucking leave before they get here."

Arnold—or whatever the fucker's name was—snorted. "Right. Guys like you never call the police. Come on now, get out, stop being a drama queen. I saw how you were looking at me. We can have fun."

It turned Nate's stomach to learn that he wasn't the asshole's first victim. The worst part was, what Arnold said really made sense: he probably really got away with this shit if the guys he coerced were too embarrassed to admit they were being molested by another man. Toxic masculinity was the worst, and Nate wasn't immune to that line of thinking, either. He was too embarrassed to call the police over something like this. He wasn't a small, defenseless woman. He was a pretty big guy. He should have been able to protect himself from assholes who couldn't take no for an answer.

Normally, he could have, but not when his vision was swimming and his cock was so hard. Fuck, what had been in that drink?

"Fuck off," Nate said, trying to focus his gaze on his phone. "I'm not sucking your cock, so you can wait until hell freezes over." He could wait. Maya would check her phone at some point when she noticed that he was missing.

Arnold let out a put-upon sigh, as if *Nate* was being the asshole here.

But then Nate heard the sound of retreating footsteps. The door opened and closed.

Nate peered at the door suspiciously, unconvinced that Arnold had really given up and left. It was entirely possible that the dick was waiting for him outside the bathroom.

Well, he would be waiting for a long time. Nate closed his eyes and breathed, trying to sober up, but whatever had been in his drink was hella strong. He didn't feel sober, his thoughts unable to focus on anything.

He wished Raffaele were here.

Nate shook his head, trying to shake off the inane thought, but that only made him dizzier. He groaned, dropping his head into his hands, feeling so damn pathetic and weak and pissed at himself for it. How had he missed that his drink had been spiked?

And why do you care that it was? said the voice at the back of his head. *Didn't you come here to get laid? Wouldn't the drugs have made things easier?*

The thought made him pause for a moment. But he pushed it away. He didn't… He didn't want to think about it.

He wished Raffaele were here.

Nate groaned again. For fuck's sake.

But the thought was impossible to push away, coming back to him. He yearned for Raffaele's insufferably self-assured attitude.

No one would dare spike Raffaele's drink. It was only losers like Nate who got into this kind of shit. Raffaele was so strong… and firm, and steady.

Nate felt wonderfully centered around him. So good. And safe.

Taken care of.

"Ugh, I need to bleach my brain," Nate muttered. "I'm just drunk. And drugged. That's it." He wasn't responsible for any weird thoughts in this state. This wasn't him. He didn't fucking need Raffaele Ferrara to come here like some knight in shining armor and save the day. For one thing, he didn't need saving. For another, Raffaele would make a terrible knight in shining armor. He was more of a dragon. A very bossy dragon. And a very hot one. Because dragons were hot. They breathed fire, so they were hot, right?

Christ, what was wrong with him? It seemed he was getting worse, not better. His vision was swimming and the nausea and inane thoughts were getting worse, too. The artificial arousal only added to his nausea. Maybe he needed to call 911.

He focused his gaze on the phone in his lap and then picked it up again. His hands were shaking. Was that a bad sign?

He tapped on his recent calls, intending to try Maya's number again, but his gaze fell on the contact below. *Satan.*

Later, Nate would blame his shaking hands for missing Maya's name.

But he had no excuse for not ending the call after he hit Raffaele's contact by mistake.

"Nate?"

It was absolutely disgusting the way he felt a little better and more focused just from hearing that low voice. Disgusting and very, very alarming.

"I…" Nate said, feeling incredibly foolish. "Never mind."

He hung up, and then groaned pitifully. What had he been thinking?

His phone went off.

Nate winced, but he knew better than to ignore the call. He answered. "Look, I'm sorry—I didn't mean to call you." He did his best not to slur and sound normal, but it probably wasn't surprising that he hadn't fooled anyone.

"What's wrong with you?" Raffaele said sharply. "Where are you?"

Nate blinked, confused, before realizing that Raffaele could likely hear the music. "In a club," he admitted. "Lush. Someone's drugged me and I don't feel too good."

Raffaele swore in Italian. "Are you safe right now?"

Nate let out a humorless chuckle, fighting another wave of nausea. "I locked myself in a bathroom stall."

"Good," Raffaele said in a clipped voice. "Don't leave. What are your symptoms?"

"Nausea," Nate said, closing his eyes. "My vision is kind of spinning. Tremors. And arousal."

There was silence on the line for a moment before Raffaele said in a rather chilling voice, "Who were you with?"

Nate opened his eyes. "Some guy at the bar," he said, feeling unsure, almost guilty. Which was ridiculous on so many levels Nate tried not to dwell on the feeling. Annoyed with himself, he said, "He was flirting with me. He wanted me to suck his cock."

"Did you." Raffaele's voice was so toneless it didn't even sound like a question.

Nate almost said yes. He wanted to say yes, just to see how Raffaele would react.

"No," he said, not offering any explanation. He didn't owe it to him. They were just the boss and his PA who fucked sometimes, nothing more. Raffaele had made it clear—and that was all Nate wanted, too. Really.

"I'll be there in fifteen minutes. Don't move."

The relief that hit him was so strong it almost made him forget about his nausea. Almost.

He opened his mouth to say thanks, but the call disconnected.

Nate closed his eyes again and prepared to wait. Just fifteen minutes. He could wait fifteen minutes. Then *he* would be here. And everything would be all right.

He didn't know how much time had passed when his phone went off again.

"Nate?" Maya said when he answered. "Where the hell are you? Did you go home with someone?"

Fighting another wave of dizziness, Nate managed, "I'm in the bathroom. Some asshole spiked my drink. I don't feel good."

"What—I'm coming!"

A few minutes later, Nate heard some guy chuckle. "This is a men's restroom."

"My brother needs my help," Maya said, undeterred. "Nate?" she said, sounding closer.

"In here," Nate forced out.

The door rattled. "Open the door, honey," Maya said.

His hands shaking, Nate reached out and unlocked the door. Or rather, tried to. His limbs felt so damn weak that even the smallest task took a lot of focus.

"Oh my god," Maya said when he finally managed to do it. "I'm calling 911."

"No," Nate said, struggling to focus his gaze on his sister. "I'm fine."

"You don't look fine! You look like you're about to pass out!"

That wasn't far from the truth, actually.

"I'm fine," Nate repeated stubbornly.

Maya sighed. "Come on, let's get you home, then." She tried to help him to his feet, but it felt like his body weighed a ton, his limbs heavy and hardly cooperating.

Nate moaned, fighting a wave of nausea. "Step back. I might throw up on you."

"Do you need help?" someone said, presumably to Maya.

"Yes, I'd appreciate that, thank you," Maya said.

And then hands—big, unfamiliar hands—touched him, trying to haul him to his feet.

Nate fought the hands. "Don't touch me!" he slurred out.

"Nate, stop that, he's just trying to help!"

"Don't need help," Nate managed, barely stopping himself from puking. Fuck, he felt so dizzy he had to close his eyes and breathe. In and out. In and out.

"Step aside," came another male voice. A very familiar, very bossy voice.

Nate breathed out. Raffaele was here. He was here. He would take care of him. Of everything.

"Wait a minute…" Maya started saying, but of course Raffaele ignored her.

Although Nate didn't open his eyes, he immediately recognized the hands on his body. He relaxed into the touch and didn't resist when Raffaele hauled him to his feet. He buried his face in his boss's neck, his hands clutching weakly at Raffaele's back. He breathed in, some of his nausea fading away when he smelled Raffaele's familiar scent. He smelled so nice. It wasn't his cologne. Just his skin.

"Can you walk?" Raffaele said.

Nate assessed his state.

"I can try," he mumbled. "Just don't let me fall."

"I won't," Raffaele said after a moment, putting Nate's arm around his shoulders. "Hold on."

Nate held on, and they started walking.

Truth be told, Raffaele had to do most of the walking. He was basically carrying Nate by the time they got out of the club.

"Our car is there," Maya's voice said. She sounded tense. Uncomfortable.

"I'll take him in my car," Raffaele said.

Nate's half-hard cock went fully hard again. "Yeah," he said, nuzzling Raffaele's neck. "Take me in your car."

"Nate!" Maya choked out, sounding a mix of scandalized, amused, and disapproving.

Nate couldn't bring himself to care. He sucked on Raffaele's neck, inhaling his scent greedily. His nausea was nearly gone, arousal pushing to the forefront of his mind. God, he wanted him. So, so much.

"Want you," he mumbled, wrapping his arms around Raffaele's neck.

Raffaele's arm around him tightened. "You're drugged," he said, his voice almost gentle.

Nate shivered, burying his face tighter against his neck. "Always want you. Only you."

Maya made another strangled noise.

"Shut up, Nate," she said. "You're going to hate yourself tomorrow."

Nate didn't care. It was suddenly of the utmost importance to tell Raffaele how much he wanted him. "Hate being away from you," he muttered, kissing Raffaele's throat. "I used to hate your horrible soul-sucking kisses, but now I want them all the time. Want you all the time. Miss sleeping next to you."

"Nate, shut up," Maya said, sounding pained.

Nate whined in protest when Raffaele gently pushed him away. "Don't go," he said, clutching at Raffaele's shirt.

"I'm not going anywhere," Raffaele said, his voice uncharacteristically patient. "But you need to get into the car. I have to drive. I can't drive with you all over me."

"No," Nate said stubbornly. "Maya can drive. You stay with me."

Raffaele sighed. "Here," he said, presumably to Maya. "You'll have to drive."

"What about Nate's car?" Maya said.

"I'll send someone to pick it up," Raffaele said.

And then Raffaele half-carried Nate into the backseat of his car and settled him against the seat. Too far. Nate made a noise of protest and buried his face in Raffaele's neck again.

"Don't puke," Raffaele told him as the car took off.

"Should we take him to the hospital?" Maya said.

"No," Nate said again.

"I think he should be fine after the drug wears off," Raffaele said after a moment. "If he doesn't get better by the morning, then take him to the hospital."

"Don't want the hospital," Nate mumbled, kissing his Adam's apple. How could a person smell so good at ass o'clock? "Want you. Only you."

"For god's sake, Nate," Maya said. "Please shut up."

Nate did shut up. He slipped his hand down Raffaele's firm chest, enjoying how strong it was, then lower, playing with the buckle of his belt.

"Nate," Raffaele said quietly, his voice not quite as steady as normal. When Nate slipped his hand lower, he found out why: the bulge straining Raffaele's pants was unmistakable. Nate groped it possessively. God, he couldn't wait to get Raffaele inside of him again.

It'd been too long. Four whole hours.

"You'd better not be touching his dick, Nate," Maya said, her voice strained.

Nate froze guiltily. How did she know? It was dark in the backseat. "Am not touching his dick," he said sulkily, putting his hand back on Raffaele's chest.

There was something soothing about the steady beat of his heart. He felt so very safe.

His eyelids grew heavier and then—nothing.

Chapter 24

Maya Parrish shot another look at the mirror and what she saw in the backseat made her purse her lips. Her little brother was sleeping like a baby, his face tucked against Raffaele Ferrara's neck and his hand clutching his shirt as if he was afraid the man would disappear. Just sex. Right.

"So," Maya said, breaking the silence. "Your relationship with my brother... what is it?"

The man's face was obscured by shadows, the streetlights occasionally illuminating his sharp, dark eyes. "My relationship?" he repeated in a vaguely mocking undertone, as if the mere concept was ridiculous. Which was kind of hilarious, considering that his hand was still cradling Nate's nape in a manner that was hard to call anything but possessive.

Jesus, this man grated on her nerves. He looked like a typical rich asshole: arrogant, proud, and so damn self-assured it was difficult not to defer to him. It annoyed Maya that she'd ended up asking for Ferrara's opinion on where to take her own brother. Nate had been right that this man was a force of nature, whether one liked him or not. It was beyond annoying.

Not to mention that she didn't like the way he touched her baby brother: with the same entitled confidence, as if it were his *right*.

"Are you going to keep fucking him until you're caught and his career is fucked, pun intended?" Maya said. "Because it's going to happen if you keep acting like such a selfish ass."

"Don't talk about things you know nothing about." Ferrara's tone was mild, but there was an icy undertone that matched well with the slight chill his presence was giving off.

Maya scoffed. "My brother told me enough. You can have anyone, Mister Billionaire. Don't you have enough supermodels to fuck? Leave Nate alone. He deserves better."

"Your brother is an adult. This is none of your business."

Maya gritted her teeth but had nothing to say to that. Her brother was an adult; he was right about that.

The rest of the drive was silent save for Nate mumbling something sleepily sometimes.

Finally, Maya parked the Maserati in front of their apartment building and led the way to their apartment while Ferrara carried her brother behind her.

"Put him on the bed," she said, entering Nate's room.

Ferrara did as he was told, but when he started straightening up, Nate made a protesting noise, his hand clutching at his shirt. "Don't go," he mumbled, his eyes still closed, his other hand sneaking up Ferrara's neck and pulling him down. "Stay," he slurred out, kissing Ferrara's jaw. "Mmm, you smell so good... Stay... Miss sleeping with you."

Maya cringed. Nate was going to be so mortified tomorrow.

"I can't stay," Ferrara said, making no actual effort to pull away and putting up with Nate's sloppy kisses all over his jaw and neck.

"Why not?" Nate whined with a pout—a *pout!*—trying to pull his boss down on top of him.

Ferrara didn't budge, his muscles locked as he eyed Nate with an expression Maya couldn't quite read.

"The bed is too small," Ferrara said, though Maya got the impression it wasn't quite what he wanted to say.

"You can sleep on top of me," Nate mumbled, his hands running up and down the older man's muscular back in such a greedy, sensual way that it made Maya blush and she wasn't even the blushing type. There were some things she didn't want to see, thanks very much. Her baby brother in a haze of lust was one of them.

"No, he *can't* sleep on top of you," Maya said firmly, stepping forward and hoping that being reminded of her presence would knock some sense into Nate and he would finally shut up.

Except Nate didn't even glance at her, his blue eyes roaming over Ferrara's face and neck in a way Maya could only describe as ravenous. It was fucking disturbing. The guy wasn't even all that handsome. All right, Ferrara was handsome, but his face wasn't really the kind that made people stare; rather, it was the type that made people avoid eye contact with him. But Nate's gaze was transfixed. Enchanted. Honestly, Maya was starting to doubt that he even registered her presence in the room.

She cleared her throat. Loudly.

Nate ignored her again. "What have you done to me?" he whispered, looking at Ferrara with his glazed blue eyes. "You're really the devil. You and your stupid shirts and ties and eyes... You turned me into—into... I shouldn't hate going home after work."

Maya could see Ferrara's face only in profile, but she

could still see that his expression became very strange.

"Feel like I'm drowning in you sometimes," Nate whispered, his words slurred and barely intelligible. "I hated you so much, but now everything feels dull without you. Want to see you always."

Dread curled in Maya's stomach. God. This was bad. She had suspected that Nate's "it's just sex" was bullshit, but this was worse than anything she had imagined. This could only end in tears. Nate's career wasn't the only thing in danger here. There was much more at stake.

She looked at Ferrara. He was still looking at Nate with that strange expression.

"I'll stay," he said, breaking the silence.

Nate gave him such a sunny, lovesick smile it made Maya a little ill. Fuck, this was bad. This was horrible. Only a blind man wouldn't see how infatuated Nate was, and she didn't think Ferrara was blind. But she couldn't read what he was thinking as Ferrara looked at Nate's smile for a moment before turning his head and looking at her.

"Leave us," he said, his expression blank. "I'll take it from here."

Maya looked uncertainly at her brother, who seemed to be just a few moments away from falling asleep. "He's drugged," she said tersely. "If you do anything to him when he's in this state—"

"I'm not going to fuck him," Ferrara stated flatly. "Now close the door from the other side."

Before she could think twice, Maya found herself obeying. She stared at the closed door in front of her and shook her head, feeling lost.

Jesus. That man really was a force of nature.

She could only hope her baby brother wouldn't be crushed under it.

Chapter 25

Raffaele watched Nate sleep.

It was possible that the drug in Nate's drink had made him confused. It was possible he had been talking nonsense.

It was also possible that pigs flew. *Enough* with excuses. Drunken ramblings should never be disregarded as unimportant. All alcohol did was loosen inhibitions. It was undeniable that Nate had some kind of *feelings* toward him. Infatuation.

Raffaele clenched his jaw, trying to ignore the storm of contradictory emotions the idea caused.

Mumbling something in his sleep, Nate moved and tucked his face against Raffaele's shoulder, slinging his leg over his thigh.

Raffaele stared at his golden eyelashes and pink, parted lips.

I hated you so much, but now everything feels dull without you. Want to see you always.

His stomach tightened with an odd, not entirely unpleasant feeling, and Raffaele's lips thinned. He should have been angry about this. Nate's idiotic feelings were going to cost Raffaele a perfectly good assistant he had gotten—used to. They'd had a good system going; why had Nate had to go and ruin it? And Nate had ruined it. Raffaele's hand was forced now.

Contrary to popular opinion, Raffaele wasn't a cruel man. He didn't enjoy breaking people's hearts.

After his last spectacular, disastrous break-up a decade ago, he'd made a rule for himself, and he'd stuck to it: no more relationships. He cut all ties to a woman if he noticed that she was starting to make moon eyes at him. It was better to break things off before there were real feelings involved and someone got hurt when he inevitably couldn't keep it in his pants and fucked someone else.

In the past, ending his association with the woman in question had been easy. All he had to do was stop having sex with her and tell his PA not to take calls from her. Heartless? Maybe. But it was practical. Kind, even—from a certain point of view.

But this time, things were more complicated. The "woman" was his PA.

Raffaele sighed heavily. Dammit, he didn't want another assistant. He was a creature of habit. He didn't want to have to train another PA.

Like that's the only reason you're stalling, a snide voice said at the back of his mind. *You should have transferred him away months ago instead of stuffing him full of your cock several times a day.*

Raffaele ran a hand over his face, exhaling through his gritted teeth. It was undeniable that the thing with Nate had lasted far longer than any of his sexual arrangements in the past decade. Nate's sister was correct that it was only a matter of time before everyone in the company found out about them fucking, and it really would ruin Nate's career before it even properly started. And he didn't want that to happen. He… he liked Nate.

The thought made Raffaele grimace, but he couldn't deny it. He liked Nate—as a person. He liked him more than he liked… pretty much everyone. It wasn't a new development.

Even back at the beginning, when Nate had grated on his nerves with his insubordination, stubbornness, and self-righteousness, he still amused Raffaele. If he hadn't liked Nate, he would have fired him a long time ago.

But he had been selfish. Selfish and greedy. He was yet to get bored of Nate; his reluctance to let him go stemmed from that.

It didn't matter.

He knew what he had to do.

Rules were rules.

And for once, he would be doing the "right thing."

***

Nate's morning didn't start well. Putting it mildly.

He had woken up to a massive headache and a very unimpressed sister who had told him things that made Nate want to never leave the bed.

"Yes, he carried you home," Maya said. "And you kept saying how much you want him, and that you miss sleeping with him, and that your life is dull and empty without him."

"Tell me you're kidding," Nate groaned into his pillow. "Please say you're pulling my leg."

"Sadly, no," Maya said. "I've never felt such second-hand embarrassment."

Nate groaned again. "Someone kill me now."

"It was embarrassing, yeah, but it's not the end of the world," his sister said. "Don't be such a drama queen. He didn't seem to take it all that badly. He even stayed with you for a while."

Nate cringed. "You just don't know him," he said miserably. "If what you're saying is true, he was likely very annoyed, but you wouldn't have noticed it. You can't read him like I can."

"Maybe. But you can't hide in your bed forever. Get up or you'll be late for work."

A long shower and a Tylenol made him feel better, and Nate felt almost normal by the time he arrived at work—if one didn't count the mortification churning in his gut.

His stomach dropped when he saw that Raffaele was already in his office. Fuck.

Okay. There was no point in delaying the inevitable, was there? If he acted like yesterday never happened, hopefully Raffaele would do the same.

Before he could do anything, the intercom clicked and Raffaele's voice said, "Nate, my office."

Taking a deep breath, Nate strode toward it. "Morning," he said, licking his lips. God, Raffaele looked so good this morning. He wanted to climb into his lap, bury his fingers into his dark hair, and kiss him.

Raffaele lifted his gaze from the document he was holding and just looked at Nate for a long moment, a very strange expression in his black eyes.

Then he pushed the document across his desk.

Frowning, Nate walked over and picked it up.

He stared at it uncomprehendingly for a few seconds. "What...?"

"You're transferred to the Game Design department," Raffaele said. "The position of a junior level designer for the next Rangers game was open, and your CV indicates that you should be well suited for it."

Nate stared at him, his mind unable to grasp what was happening.

"You're firing me?" he finally managed.

"Hardly. This is a promotion." Raffaele's face was completely unreadable. "Isn't it what you always wanted? You always made it clear that you didn't want to be my PA. This is your reward for putting up with the job you hated for nine months. You're a level designer on your favorite game now, effective immediately. Congratulations."

Effective immediately?

"But..." Nate couldn't think. "But I haven't found you another PA yet."

"It doesn't matter," Raffaele said, shifting his gaze to his computer. "I already told HR to find me a new PA. Speaking of... They're waiting for you to sign your new contract. You may go."

Nate opened his mouth and then closed it when nothing came out. He didn't know what to say. What to think. How to feel.

He should have been happy, right? This was his dream job, on his favorite franchise. This really was an incredible opportunity.

But.

Level designers worked on the second floor. They might as well be on another planet from the top floor where the executives' offices were located. Only heads of the departments ever came here. It was glaringly obvious why he was being transferred there. Raffaele didn't want to see him again.

Swallowing the sudden tightness in his throat, Nate curled his lips into a smile. "Thanks for the opportunity. Sir."

Raffaele lifted his gaze.

Their eyes locked.

Something shifted in Raffaele's—*Ferrara's* expression, his mouth tightening.

"It's for the best," he said in a clipped voice. "Good luck in your new job."

"Thank you," Nate said with a wide smile that made his cheeks ache. "Sir."

He turned swiftly and walked out of the room.

He didn't slam the door on his way out. He wanted to, but he wouldn't give him the satisfaction.

He closed it, very carefully.

Chapter 26

The new PA, Martin Baddock, was perfect. He was excellent at everything he did. Raffaele's shirts were always perfectly ironed, the tasks he gave were completed to perfection, and his schedule was better structured than it had ever been.

The sight of him still irritated Raffaele to an unhealthy degree.

He should have been used to the guy by now. Martin had been his PA for nearly two months now. He was excellent at his job. Raffaele had nothing to complain about—rationally. Irrationally, everything about Martin made him angry, even his obedient attitude and brown hair.

At first Raffaele had thought it was just sexual frustration. Except the moment his new PA had helpfully offered to call an escort service for him, Raffaele had nearly bitten off his head. He didn't want a paid whore. Nate would have known better than to suggest that. Nate would have rolled his eyes and made some insolent remark about his horniness before getting to his knees and wrapping his lovely lips around his cock—

Raffaele pinched the bridge of his nose. He really needed to get laid. It had been two months since he'd had sex—something completely unheard of for him. His right hand wasn't taking the edge off anymore, and the constant hum of sexual frustration under his skin was seriously interfering with his focus at work.

It was an easily fixable issue. Supposed to be.

Except he didn't want just any hole around his cock. He'd already tried using one of his booty calls, and even thinking about that attempt made him grimace now. The woman, Clarisse, was gorgeous. Physically, his body had found her attractive, but the moment she climbed into his lap and attempted to kiss him, he had stopped her. He had no idea why. He just hadn't wanted to fuck her or kiss her or touch her. He'd sent her away, feeling even more frustrated and irritated than he had been.

It made no sense. He'd never been all that selective. His high libido normally ensured that he didn't even care much about his sex partners' physical appearance: plump or skinny, blonde or brunette—it had made no difference to him. Sex was just sex. A warm body was a warm body.

Until now, apparently.

But then again, now he was doing so many things he'd never done before.

Like spying on his employees.

Pressing his lips together, Raffaele clicked the mouse, opening the live feed from the second floor. It didn't take him long to zoom in on the right cubicle. Nate was seated at his workstation, his gaze on his computer, typing fast. His brows were furrowed in concentration, and he was chewing on his bottom lip thoughtfully. He looked good. A little tired, judging by the dark circles under his eyes, but good.

Raffaele stared at him greedily. He felt like the worst sort of creep, but he couldn't bring himself to close the video.

Somehow, the boring sight of Nate typing was far more arousing than the sight of Clarisse's naked body. What was wrong with him, fucking hell.

Closing his eyes, Raffaele pinched the bridge of his nose again.

This... obsession was getting out of hand. It had been two months. He should have forgotten about the boy a long time ago instead of stalking him at work like a creep, as if he didn't have a hundred other things to do.

Maybe he just needed to talk to him. Get some closure.

Maybe the problem was that Nate hadn't really reacted in the way Raffaele had half-expected him to react when he had told him about the job transfer. If he were honest with himself, he had... he had expected that Nate would try to convince him otherwise. Nate had had feelings for him. Hadn't he been supposed to show some emotion when Raffaele broke things off?

Raffaele opened his eyes, disturbed by his strange train of thought. Had he actually *wanted* Nate to be clingy?

No, surely not.

He returned his gaze to the screen. Nate was talking to the woman from the cubicle to his left. Smiling at her. They laughed together, the woman's eyes fixed on Nate's smiling lips.

A snap caught his attention, and Raffaele looked down. The pen in his hand had snapped and he now had purple ink all over his fingers. He threw the pen away in disgust.

He opened the second drawer of his desk, but the wet wipes weren't there. Nate had always put them there.

The intercom chimed. "Sir, HR wants to speak to you about the crunch issue," Martin said.

"Where are the wet wipes?" Raffaele growled.

"Um—wet wipes?" Martin stammered. "The th-third drawer, sir."

"They're supposed to be in the second one," he bit off, yanking the third drawer open and glaring at the offending things. He grabbed one and wiped his fingers.

After a long silence, Martin said hesitantly, "What about HR, sir?"

"I'm busy. Tell them I'm unavailable."

"Of course, sir," Martin said.

Nate wouldn't have agreed so timidly. He would have been indignant on behalf of people he didn't even know.

Raffaele grimaced, pushing the thought out of his mind. Could he not think of his ex-PA for five damn minutes?

Fuck. Clearly something needed to be done.

He pressed the intercom button. "Martin, connect me to Level Design. I want to speak to Nate Parrish."

"Of course, sir."

On the screen, Nate finally turned away from that woman and picked up the phone in a rather distracted manner. He could see Nate freeze, his pretty blue eyes widening when he was likely told who wanted to speak to him. He watched Nate's Adam's apple bob. Then Nate said something and Martin's voice sounded again, "I'm putting Nate Parrish through, sir."

And then Nate's voice said, "Hello?"

He sounded hesitant. He looked confused, his mouth opening and closing. Fuck, Raffaele wanted to shove his tongue into that pretty mouth and kiss him until he couldn't breathe. *Focus, dammit.*

"I can't find the AK Media file," he said tersely and then grimaced, aware how abrupt and strange it must have sounded, without any kind of greeting.

"The AK Media file?" Nate repeated, his brows

furrowing. "I don't remember that company."

Of course he didn't. Raffaele had just made it up.

"Come here and find it for me," Raffaele said before he could stop himself.

Nate wet his lips with his pink tongue, and Raffaele pressed the heel of his hand against his erection.

"Don't you have a new personal slave to do that job for you?" Nate said. "I have my job to do, Mr. Ferrara."

That little—

"I'm still your boss," Raffaele said.

"You're my boss's boss," Nate said, leaning back in his chair and closing his eyes. "I don't answer to you anymore. I answer to Jordan Gates."

Raffaele narrowed his eyes. Jordan Gates, the Lead Designer, was a handsome man in his early thirties. He was recently divorced and supposedly straight, but that didn't mean anything. Raffaele had been as straight as they came, and yet here he was, obsessing over another man and getting a hard-on just from hearing his voice and looking at him. He would have to monitor Jordan Gates, make sure that he—

Get a grip, he told himself, deeply unsettled by the direction of his thoughts. It was bad enough that he was acting like an obsessed, creepy stalker; he drew the line at behaving like a possessive psychopath.

"Is there anything else you wanted, Mr. Ferrara?" Nate said in the same nauseatingly detached tone of voice.

Raffaele clenched his jaw. Had he really gotten over him so fast? What happened to "the world feels dull without you"?

"Nothing," he bit out, closing the video, and hung up.

He was in an utterly foul mood for the rest of the day.

Chapter 27

Nate loved his new job. It was challenging and new and definitely not easy, but he was finally working on something he was passionate about. His co-workers were nice, and his boss was... well, maybe not "nice," but nice enough compared to—

Anyway. He was doing well. He loved his job. Life was good.

Of course it had taken only one call to ruin everything.

Nate pursed his lips, thinking once again about Raffaele's call last week. Hearing his voice again had felt like a punch to the gut: it had left him breathless and his body hot and full of adrenaline. He had felt so damn alive. Not that he had felt dead in the past few months, but the world was suddenly so much brighter and more vibrant, and hearing Raffaele's voice was just... Nate talked to him mechanically, hardly knowing what he said, hearing his own voice as though it were someone else's. It'd taken all his willpower to refuse when Raffaele ordered him to come up to him. But god, he had wanted to go, so badly. Just to see him. Take that excuse to see him and be around him, and—

Fucking pathetic. He was so pathetic. The asshole had basically discarded him like used goods, and yet here he was, still pining for crumbs of his attention. He was better than that, dammit.

A wave of whispers rolled through the large room, snapping him out of his thoughts.

Nate looked up. He couldn't see much from his cubicle, but he could see that his co-workers were suddenly sitting very straight, giving off the *I'm-working-so-hard* vibe.

That kind of reaction was... familiar. Only one man usually caused it.

Nate shivered, his heart jumping into his throat. His stomach clenched when he heard murmurs of "Mr. Ferrara" and "Sir."

Nate fixed his gaze on his computer, putting on a busy appearance and trying to ignore the way his stomach was full of butterflies. Horrible, flesh-eating butterflies.

He was being stupid. There was no damn way Raffaele was here to see him. He probably had a meeting with Nate's boss, though that would be pretty strange, too. Usually department heads went up to the executive floor, not vice versa. Raffaele Ferrara usually didn't deign to grace the mere mortals with his presence unless there was an emergency. In fact, Nate could count on his fingers the number of times it had happened since he'd started working for the Caldwell Group almost a year ago.

Footsteps stopped right next to his cubicle.

Fuck, Nate couldn't fight it anymore.

Slowly, he lifted his gaze.

He was glad that he was sitting, because his knees were suddenly weak when his eyes locked with Raffaele's. He couldn't fucking breathe.

He was wearing a blue tie today. It looked ridiculously good against Raffaele's smooth, gorgeous olive skin, drawing one's gaze to the cleft on his chin and his firm, sensual lips.

Nate licked his own. He'd always rolled his eyes when people described want and desire in terms of "hunger," but he felt hungry now. Starved.

His mouth was tingling, watering. He wanted to launch himself at Raffaele and *eat* him. It was a visceral feeling, raw and powerful. It left Nate dizzy. Famished.

"Sir," he heard himself say. He sounded surprisingly normal and not at all like he was gripping his chair hard in order to stop himself from jumping his boss in front of everyone and climbing him like a tree.

Raffaele didn't say anything for a moment, just looking at him with that hard, intense look of his that was achingly familiar. Nate had almost forgotten how warm and hyperaware of himself that look made him feel, as if he were the only thing in the world.

"How are you doing?" Raffaele said.

Nate blinked, still gripping the chair as if his life depended on it. "I'm—I'm good. The job is great! I like it a lot." Fuck, could he sound more awkward? In his defense, he wasn't used to making small talk with his boss—the boss he used to fuck—while his co-workers pretended not to be listening to every word.

"I'm glad," Raffaele said stiffly. "Is Jordan in his office?"

"I think so," Nate said, his stomach sinking. Of course Raffaele hadn't come to see him. Of course he was here on business.

Giving a clipped nod, Raffaele strode away and disappeared into Nate's boss's office.

Nate sagged, feeling like all the tension bled out of his body. He'd never felt so elated and disappointed at the same time—elated that he'd seen him and disappointed that Raffaele hadn't come here for him. He was an idiot, yes.

"Oof," Camilla said from the cubicle to his left. "I've never seen the boss here. Do you think there's trouble?"

Nate shrugged and fixed his gaze on his computer.

He didn't look up when Raffaele emerged out of the office, deep in conversation with Jordan, but he followed them with his eyes as soon as they passed his cubicle.

His stomach twisted unpleasantly when he saw Jordan's blond head so close to Raffaele's dark one. He was being stupid. Yes, Jordan Gates was handsome, but that didn't mean that Raffaele wanted to fuck him. He was straight.

Right, his inner voice said snidely. *Do you think you were that special? If he fucked you, he might want to fuck Jordan, too. You look kind of alike.*

Nate pressed his lips together, hating the direction of his thoughts, but he couldn't stop them. Jordan's height and build really were similar to his. His hair was slightly darker, closer to dirty blond. His eyes were blue, too, but they were nothing like his own: so pale they seemed colorless and emotionless. Jordan was objectively very handsome, but he wasn't the type to smile much. To be honest, the guy kind of intimidated Nate. He didn't find him attractive at all. It didn't mean that Raffaele wouldn't, though.

His mood souring, Nate shifted his gaze back to his computer.

"It's none of my business," he muttered under his breath.

"What?" Camilla said.

"Nothing."

***

Raffaele came back two days later.

And then the next day, too.

The whole department was buzzing, nervous that something was up.

"Maybe there are layoffs coming up," Toby said after Raffaele left.

Everyone glared at him, but from the expressions on people's faces they were afraid of the same thing.

"It's not that," Nate said, shaking his head. "He never gets personally involved in layoffs."

"God, I forget that you were his PA," Susan said with a chuckle. "Can't you ask him what's up?"

"Yeah," Toby said, looking at Nate curiously. "He always stops at your desk. What do you talk about?"

"Nothing," Nate said.

"Oh, come on!"

"He's telling the truth," Camilla chimed in. "They make some small talk and then he leaves. It's super boring."

Nate pulled a face. She was right though. On the three occasions Raffaele had come to their department, all they exchanged were a few stilted words between long silences. It was the definition of awkward.

The worst part was, Nate fucking lived for those few minutes. He hated the way his heart tried to beat out of his chest when Raffaele looked at him, the way his stomach seemed to be full of butterflies, and his face was too warm and everything was too much. The moment Raffaele left, he felt almost nauseated from the crash of adrenaline and disappointment.

He'd never felt this way, not even when he had been a teenager.

Nate had no idea what to do. The feelings he'd been trying to suppress so hard when they had been fucking seemed to become a thousand times worse now that he couldn't even touch Raffaele's *hand*. He felt like there was a hole inside him, yearning. Thirsty. He felt like an addict who could see his fix but wasn't allowed to have it. It got to the point that he couldn't string two thoughts together after he saw Raffaele and was only capable of monosyllabic answers for the rest of the day, too distracted and keyed up.

It couldn't keep going that way; Nate knew it. It didn't help that with Raffaele's every visit to Jordan, Nate's suspicions about the nature of those visits grew into something ugly and sickening. He wasn't usually one to hate anyone for no reason, but he couldn't stand the sight of his boss now. He hated Jordan's immaculate suits, handsome face and confidence. He hated his nicely shaped lips and pale eyes that betrayed nothing, no matter how hard Nate looked at him after Raffaele's visits.

"Nate, my office," came Jordan's voice over the intercom. Speak of the devil.

"What does he want?" Camilla said.

Shrugging, Nate got up and strode toward Jordan's office. He pushed the door open.

"You wanted to see me?" he said, keeping his voice carefully neutral. Hopefully it wasn't obvious that he couldn't stand the guy.

Jordan regarded him for a long moment before before saying, "Make Ferrara stop coming here."

"What?"

"You heard me. His presence disrupts everyone's work, including mine."

"What does it have to do with me?" Nate said with a chuckle.

"Don't insult my intelligence. He's never paid so much attention to my department—until he transferred you here."

"I really don't understand what you're implying," Nate managed, his heart beating faster and his palms growing sweaty.

The look Jordan fixed him with was distinctly unimpressed. "I don't give a fuck if you sucked his cock to get this job," he said flatly. "You're capable of your job and you get things done—that's the part I care about. But I don't want Ferrara's extra scrutiny on us. Everyone is saying that there must be something wrong with my department if the boss is paying so much attention to it. Get him off my back."

"I..." Nate ran a hand over his warm face. Although he was kind of mortified, the prevalent emotion he felt was relief. So Raffaele wasn't actually fucking Jordan. "I really don't have any influence over him. Look, you're wrong. He isn't here because of me."

Jordan scoffed. "Please. I knew something was up when he transferred you here and gave you a salary three times higher than a junior level designer without much experience normally gets—"

"He did?" Nate said faintly, his brows drawing close. He'd been pleasantly surprised by the salary when he'd signed the contract, but he'd thought nothing of it.

"I don't know what he wants, but give it to him," Jordan said shortly, pushing his thin glasses up the bridge of his nose. "I'd suck his cock myself if it were what he wanted, but it clearly isn't."

Nate stared at him.

"I thought you were straight," he said awkwardly.

Jordan snorted. "I am."

Right. Because that totally made sense.

But Nate didn't dare question him on that. Jordan was still his boss, no matter how candidly he was talking now. And the guy was still intimidating as hell, the look of his pale blue eyes more than a little unnerving.

"I'll think about it," Nate said instead, before turning and leaving.

He did think about it. It was all he thought about for the rest of the day, and during his drive home.

"What's with the long face?" Maya said when she saw him.

Pacing the room, Nate told her everything: about Raffaele's weird visits, his conversation with Jordan, the salary thing too.

When he was done talking, he found a resigned look on his sister's face.

"What?" Nate said, stopping his pacing.

"What do you want, Nate?" she said quietly.

He frowned. "I don't understand."

Maya heaved a sigh. "You've been obsessed with that asshole for a year now. I was hoping you'd get over him when he actually did something decent and gave you the job you deserve, but you've been moping for months—"

"I haven't been moping!"

"Please," Maya said. "You put up a pretty good front and pretended that you were excited about the new job, but I know you. Your eyes were sad. Even Mom noticed that."

"What? What did she say? I am excited about the job. And my eyes weren't *sad*!"

Maya rolled her eyes. "They were—they have been for months. Mom asked me if you had a recent breakup. I said yes, because you know what? That's actually pretty accurate. You broke up with the guy your life had revolved around for the better part of a year."

Nate opened his mouth and then closed it without saying anything. There was nothing to say.

"You looked like you'd cry if I talked about him, so I left it alone, figuring that you'd get better after a while. And although you didn't turn into a depressed wreck, it was as if…as if you were muted. I haven't seen you this excited about anything in months. When a few days ago you got home looking animated again, I thought you were finally over him, but apparently it was the opposite and you just saw him again." Maya shook her head with a crooked smile. "Look, I give up. You know I've never liked that guy, but if just seeing him can put that look into your eyes, I give up. An idiot in love is better than the sad-eyed zombie you've been."

"I wasn't—I'm not—"

"What, not in love with him?" Maya said, giving him a flat look.

Nate swallowed. "Maybe just a little infatuated," he said in a small voice.

Maya let out an inelegant snort. "I think that ship sailed back when you were ranting to me about how much you hated him, well before you started sucking his cock. You were obsessed with him even back then. All you talked about was him."

Fuck, she had a point.

Looking back, Nate couldn't even tell when he had stopped hating Raffaele. The emotions Raffaele had caused in him had always been so intense that he hadn't even noticed when his feelings shifted into something other than hatred. It was a gradual thing, so it was something he hadn't been aware of until it was too late. Or maybe he'd just been in denial about it. Because the hurt, the heartache he felt when Raffaele had told him that he was being transferred to another department didn't fit the word infatuation.

He'd known that, but he'd pushed those thoughts away and suppressed the hell out of them. Because it was beyond stupid to fall in love with a man like Raffaele Ferrara.

In love. Love.

Shit.

Nate sat down heavily on the couch, dropping his head into his hands. "Fuck."

Maya sighed, wrapping an arm around his shoulders. "Chin up. It's not the end of the world."

"You don't understand," he said with a humorless laugh. "Raffaele doesn't do relationships. Ever. He's the worst person I could fall in love with. All he wants is meaningless sex."

"If all he wanted was meaningless sex, he has a funny way of showing it."

"What do you mean?" Nate said, lifting his head.

Maya shrugged slightly. "The guy gave you a ridiculously high salary for your new job, didn't even ask for his car back—"

"He's so rich it doesn't mean anything, Maya," Nate said, shaking his head. He frowned a little. "But I should return the car. I'd completely forgotten about it."

Liar, a voice said at the back of his mind. *You hoped it would give him a reason to call you.*

"Fine," Maya said. "Maybe money means nothing to him, so it doesn't necessarily mean he cares about you. But why is he stalking your workplace, then? Admit it: it's weird. Even your boss thinks he's coming there because of you."

Nate looked away, frowning. It *was* weird. And very out of character. It wasn't like Raffaele to waste what little time he had on personally monitoring a small department of the company. Nate knew better than anyone how insane Raffaele's workload was. It just didn't add up.

"What, you think he misses me or something?" Nate said with a laugh, trying to quash the stupid hope that was now burning in his chest.

"Do you have any other explanation?" Maya said. "He's hot, and he's a billionaire. He can have anyone for meaningless sex. Why would he waste his time on making awkward small talk with you in front of everyone if he just wanted to get his dick wet?"

"Maya."

She chuckled. "What? I'm just saying it how it is. You know I'm far from being his fan, but I think you're being unfair to him."

She pulled a funny face. "Yeah, I can't believe I just said that. I think he's clearly trying to—to connect with you, but he has no idea how to do it when he can't boss you around or order you to suck his cock. If he doesn't do relationships, he's clearly out of his comfort zone, hence the stalking, staring, and awkward small talk."

Nate just looked at her, at a loss.

Could she be right?

"But that's not the important thing. The important thing is what *you* want. What do you want, Nate?"

"I don't understand."

"God, *men*," Maya said, shaking her head. Then she looked back at him. "Do you want a relationship with him? You know all his horrible qualities and habits, his commitment issues. And he's still your boss—and everything that entails. Do you want him that badly?"

Nate stared at her.

His heart sank, because the answer to the question was *yes*. He didn't even have to think about it.

The answer must have been written all over his face, because she sighed again and, taking his hand, squeezed it. "Then get him. But don't let him have the upper hand. He's not the boss of you anymore—" She made a face. "Well, he's still the big boss, but you're not his direct subordinate anymore. Make him work for it. Make him woo you. And for god's sake, don't have sex with him until he proves it's not the only thing he wants."

"What?" Nate said miserably.

She laughed, rolling her eyes. "Men," she said again. "You lived without his cock for months. You can live without it for a few more."

Groaning, Nate buried his face in his hands. "You really overestimate my self-control."

Maya just laughed again.

"It's not funny," Nate grumbled. "Even if you're right and he actually still wants me, he'd never agree to a relationship without sex. Hell, I wouldn't agree to it, either! I don't know how to be around him and not want him."

"First World problems," Maya said, her voice practically dripping with sarcasm. "There's more to a relationship than sex, Nate. Maybe no sex would actually be good for you, too. Your relationship with him started totally backwards. Instead of going on dates and getting to know each other like normal people, you went straight to sex, and feelings were kind of an accident."

"I know him plenty well," Nate said sulkily. "I know him better than anyone in the world." He wasn't bragging. He used to obsess over every infinitesimal change in Raffaele's expression or the tone of his voice. Even when Nate had thought he hated him, Raffaele was still his favorite thing to look at. He loved watching him think and—

Nate's thoughts halted, his eyes going wide. Fuck, he really loved him. He loved Raffaele.

"All right, maybe you know him," Maya conceded. "But does he know you? And I don't mean in the Biblical sense."

Nate pursed his lips, unsure. "I have no idea."

"Then find out. But under no circumstances have sex with him. Get it?"

"Right," Nate said, averting his gaze.

Chapter 28

Maya's words had seemed so convincing when she had talked to him, but the more Nate thought about it, the more unbelievable they seemed. The concept of Raffaele possibly having *feelings* for him seemed so far-fetched. Laughable.

Nate still couldn't stop thinking about it over the weekend, overanalyzing every word, every look, and every touch. He knew he was obsessing. He knew he was being kind of pathetic, searching for any sign that his sister might be correct.

To be fair, there *were* things about Raffaele's behavior that had made him wonder sometimes. He'd had sex only with Nate for months, not even glancing at other people—beautiful women—with any interest. There was also the fact that he sometimes seemed kind of possessive of him. Or the fact that he had actually listened to Nate sometimes—like that time Raffaele had refused to waste his time on Andrew Reyes until Nate told him to stop being a dick. It might seem like a small thing, but Raffaele didn't allow his employees to talk to him that way, much less listen to them when they talked to him that way. Nate had always been the exception. It definitely was strange, but…

But it still seemed like a bit of a stretch to assume that Raffaele might actually have serious feelings for him. He had been the one to end things, the one who had cast Nate aside.

Nate would be damned if he behaved like those clingy women who constantly called Raffaele and refused to let go. He had his pride, dammit.

The doorbell rang, snapping Nate out of his gloomy thoughts. He looked at the door from his sprawl on the couch, wondering if Maya had forgotten her keys. But it was a little too early for her to come back from her outing with her friends.

Sighing, he got to his feet and went to open the door. Raffaele stood on the other side.

Nate's heart jumped to his throat, his mind going blank.

"What are you doing here?" he finally managed, his voice sounding surprisingly steady. He felt... He felt woefully underdressed and unattractive in his old, ratty t-shirt and equally ratty shorts, while Raffaele looked mouthwateringly good, as usual. God, he wanted to kiss him all over—the cleft in his chin, his muscular neck, his *mouth*—

Nate snapped his gaze up to Raffaele's eyes, but it was almost worse. Those black eyes burned him.

Raffaele said nothing.

Seconds ticked by, stretching into a small eternity.

Nate searched for something to say, desperate to break the silence.

"It's good that you're here, actually," he said, turning away to grab the car keys on the shelf. His fingers were trembling, fuck. "I've been meaning to return your car, but it keeps slipping my mind." He turned back and handed him the keys.

His hand hung in the air between them for a long second before Raffaele finally accepted the keys. Their fingers didn't brush.

Fuck, Nate had never wanted to grab someone's hand so badly.

"You don't have to return it," Raffaele said.

"It's your car," Nate said, unable to look him in the eye. "You should give it to your new PA." The words tasted like ash in his mouth, and he hoped his face didn't betray the ugly feeling they caused inside him. Christ, jealousy was such a horrible feeling, and a completely irrational one. Why the hell was he jealous of the poor guy who slaved as Raffaele's PA in his stead? It made no sense.

Raffaele remained silent, just looking at him.

Nate licked his lips, the pulse in his neck racing. "I… So why are you here?"

Raffaele stepped forward.

Swallowing reflexively, Nate stepped back.

The door shut, the finality of it oddly comforting and frightening at the same time. They were alone. In an apartment with a bed. And a couch. And the floor.

Get a grip.

Nate cleared his throat a little, avoiding Raffaele's gaze. He didn't trust himself. "You didn't answer."

"You did something to me."

Nate looked back at Raffaele, too startled to be flustered. "What?"

Raffaele's expression was a little tight. Grim. "You did something to me," he repeated, his voice strained. Accusing.

"What are you talking about?"

Raffaele grabbed him and then shoved Nate against the door.

Nate yelped, disoriented. His protests died on his lips when Raffaele bracketed him with his arms on either side, his eyes boring a hole in him, his expression so intense it stole Nate's breath. He should probably have been nervous, but all he could focus on was how good Raffaele smelled. How close he was. How much he missed him.

"You turned me into an idiot."

Nate blinked when the words registered.

What?

But before he could say anything, Raffaele gripped his chin with his hand and tipped his face up. He glared at Nate, his black eyes roaming over his face like a scalding, physical touch. "I can't fucking focus on my work," he ground out. "I'm either thinking of you or trying not to think of you. When I'm not stalking you through security cameras, I somehow end up on the second floor, and then I have to come up with ridiculous excuses for being there." He chuckled, the sound devoid of amusement. "This is not me. I feel like a goddamn idiot—but I can't stop."

Nate stared at him.

And then, a slow smile tugged at his lips. Stalking him through security cameras?

Really?

"It isn't funny," Raffaele bit out, a muscle ticking in his jaw. The expression on his face was so resentful that Nate's smile faded.

He loved this man. He didn't want to make his life miserable.

"Do you want me to quit?" Nate said softly.

The look Raffaele gave him was almost hateful. "No," he said, his hand moving lower and wrapping around Nate's throat. Fuck, it should have been scary, not hot. "Don't you dare."

"Then what do you want from me?" Nate whispered. His heart was pounding so fast he thought it might just burst right out of his chest.

Raffaele's grip on Nate's throat adjusted, becoming more of a caress, his thumb pressing against Nate's racing pulse.

Nate wet his dry lips with his tongue. He could taste the tension in the air, so thick and suffocating that Nate could barely breathe. He wanted to be kissed. He wanted to have Raffaele's mouth on him so badly he was trembling with it. *Please.*

But he wouldn't kiss him first. He didn't want to pressure Raffaele into something he would resent. He could feel that Raffaele wanted him—could read it in the enormous tension in his body, in the way he looked at Nate as if he were thirsty. But physical want wasn't enough for him. Nate wanted Raffaele to want *them*. To make a choice that had nothing to do with lust.

Nate lifted his hand and cupped Raffaele's stubbled cheek. God. It felt so good to touch him, after months of nothing. "I missed you, you know."

Raffaele's dark eyes glinted with a strange light. "Did you?"

Nate nodded with a rueful smile, barely able to hold his gaze. "I know you don't want to hear that—"

"No," Raffaele said, his throat bobbing up and down. "Say it."

Nate stared at him. "You actually want me to tell you how much I missed you?"

There was something greedy in Raffaele's eyes as he gave a tight nod.

A laugh left Nate's mouth. "You're such an asshole. You don't do relationships, but you want me to miss you. You do realize how messed-up it is, right?"

Raffaele's expression flickered between several emotions before settling on something like irritation.

"It's your fault."

"It's my fault that you want me to miss you," Nate stated, shooting him an incredulous look.

"Yes," Raffaele said testily, glancing down at his lips before wrenching his gaze away. His lips thinned. "You make me want things I've never wanted before."

Nate's foolish heart soared. "Like what?"

Inhaling unsteadily, Raffaele pressed his face against Nate's cheek. Nuzzled into it.

A small whine left Nate's mouth, his eyes slipping shut. God, this man. His scent...

"I want you to miss me every minute I'm not there," Raffaele said in a barely audible, hoarse whisper, mouthing the side of his face, nipping along his jaw. "Want you to think of me all the time. Only me."

"God, you're such a selfish dick," Nate said with a breathless chuckle. His face was tingling from Raffaele's mouth, and he wanted to turn his head and crush their mouths together so badly he was shaking with it.

"But you have feelings for me," Raffaele stated, his voice low and tight, kissing all over his cheek. "You love me. Admit it."

"I should fucking punch you," Nate said, trying to open his eyes but unable to do so. "You're such a smug, conceited—"

"You love me." Raffaele sucked a bruise on his jawline.

Nate let out a shuddering breath, barely stopping himself from moaning.

"Say it," Raffaele said. *Ordered.*

It made Nate's knees weak. "I love you," he mumbled, incoherent with want. "I love you. You're an asshole, but I love you—"

Raffaele seized his face and kissed him.

Gasping, Nate kissed him back, grabbing fistfuls of Raffaele's hair and moaning in *pleasure-hunger-relief.* God, finally. He couldn't kiss him hard enough, couldn't get close enough to him, he wanted to crawl inside this man, feel the warmth of his flesh and the solidity of his muscles against him. He needed him, he missed him so much, he wanted him inside of him, now—

Nate wrenched his mouth away. "Wait, we can't."

Breathing hard, Raffaele pressed their foreheads together, his body rigid with tension. "Why the hell not?"

Nate made a miserable noise. "Maya would kill me."

"What does your sister have to do with anything?" Raffaele said, mouthing the side of his face and nipping along his jawline before sucking on Nate's trembling bottom lip.

It took Nate a moment to remember what they were talking about. "I promised her I wouldn't have sex with you until you prove that you have—that you have feelings for me."

Raffaele chuckled against his mouth. "Didn't I just tell you that you make me act like an idiot?"

Nate snorted. "Is that your idea of a love confession?" Unable to help himself, he pulled Raffaele into another kiss. Just a short one. *God, Raffaele's mouth.* Its intensity was horribly addictive. He couldn't get enough of this man, he felt like he'd been famished for months.

"How about this," Raffaele said between kisses. "I haven't fucked anyone since you. I didn't even want to."

Oh.

"Really?" Nate said breathlessly, his eyes flying open. "But it's been months. You become an enormous dick if you don't get laid for a few days."

Raffaele smiled ruefully and said in a sardonic undertone, "Let's just say people are starting to hide when they see me coming."

Nate rolled his eyes. "How many people have you fired?" To his disgust, he sounded *fond* instead of exasperated or disapproving. God, he needed help.

"Very few, actually," Raffaele said. "Every time I want to fire someone, I hear your lecture in my head about poor people needing their jobs. It's extremely aggravating."

Nate grinned, looping his arms around his neck. "Now that might be love," he said and kissed him needily, pressing himself flush against him. Just one little kiss. Just one more. God, he wanted to glue himself to this man and never, ever part from him.

He honestly wasn't sure how "just one more kiss" ended up with him naked on his bed, with Raffaele's equally naked body on top of him. He didn't care, he couldn't stop, moaning against Raffaele's mouth, running his hands over Raffaele's muscular back, and spreading his legs shamelessly. He wanted to get fucked. He wanted Raffaele inside of him, wanted him closer, tighter, wanted to have him so deep he'd never get out of him.

"Come on, just put it in," he growled in frustration, gripping Raffaele's muscular buttocks and spreading his legs wider. He probably looked like a slut, but he didn't give a shit. He *was* a slut for this man. Fingers weren't enough. He wanted his cock.

Raffaele exhaled, his body rigid with tension. "I don't have a condom—"

"Don't care," Nate said, grabbing Raffaele's hard cock and guiding it between his legs. "Wanna feel you. Get in me. Give me your cock."

Raffaele shuddered. "Are you sure?"

"Yes, damn you. Now put it in." He didn't care how irresponsible it was. He wanted. He didn't want anything separating them. He wanted to feel Raffaele come. He wanted to be gross with Raffaele's bodily fluids inside and out. The mere idea of being full of another man's jizz probably shouldn't have turned him on so much, but fuck, it totally did, his own cock heavy and hard between his legs.

When Raffaele finally pushed inside him, thick and slick with lube, the noise Nate made didn't even sound human. He cried out, pushing back onto the cock, his legs wrapping tightly around Raffaele's hips and urging him on. He was so full, it felt so damn perfect, to finally have that cock where it belonged.

Raffaele thrust hard into him, his black eyes glazed, the muscles of his neck tense as he clearly tried to stop himself from coming too early. Nate drank in the sight of him, feeling so damn enamored he didn't know what to do with himself. Fuck, if Raffaele hadn't had sex in months, he must have been on edge already, but he was trying to hold himself back, stroking Nate's cock in time with his thrusts and wanting to make it good for him.

"I missed you," Nate babbled, incoherent. "Missed feeling you in me." He squeezed around the thick cock in him. "Want you to come in me. Come in me, fill me up."

Raffaele groaned, his eyes wild and dark, his hips thrusting once, twice, and then he was spilling inside him, filling him up, his muscular body shuddering.

Fuck, it was so hot, the hottest thing he'd ever seen. It took only a few strokes of his aching cock for Nate to come, too, his long moan swallowed by Raffaele's greedy mouth.

Raffaele's arms gave out, the weight of him so very comforting and familiar. So perfect.

Nate hugged him tightly, pressing their flushed cheeks together and just breathing him in as their hearts hammered against each other. He'd never felt so euphoric.

So good.

So whole.

"Maya is going to smack me for this and call me an idiot," Nate said with a chuckle, kissing Raffaele's stubbled cheek. *I love you*, his heart beat. *I love you, I love you, I love you.*

"I still can't believe you gossip with your sister about me," Raffaele said, laying his head on Nate's pillow.

Nate smiled, threading his fingers through Raffaele's damp hair. "If I didn't, I wouldn't have realized how bad I had it for you. She's the one who helped me figure things out."

"Hm. You should send her flowers from me, then."

Nate looked at him carefully.

Their faces were so close on the pillow that Nate could see every imperfection on Raffaele's face: the tiny crows feet, the deep wrinkle between his brows, the small scar above his left eye.

"I'm not returning to my former job, you know that, right?" Nate said quietly, stroking the wrinkle between Raffaele's brows with his thumb. "I know you transferred me because my drunken confession freaked you out, but you actually chose a great department for me. I like my new job."

"I know," Raffaele said, putting a heavy hand on Nate's side.

Nate barely resisted the urge to squirm even closer to him. This was important.

He couldn't get distracted.

"Really?"

"I didn't choose a job for you randomly." Raffaele's lips curled into a wry smile. "You ranted about Rangers 5's flawed level design so many times I knew you'd like an opportunity to work on the level design of the next game."

Nate blinked, touched and a little surprised that Raffaele had actually paid attention to his rants. Most people didn't, just rolling their eyes when something set off Nate's favorite topic. Maybe Raffaele did know him, after all.

"Yeah, it's my dream job," Nate said, stroking Raffaele's bicep with his knuckles. His fingers looked awfully pale against Raffaele's gorgeous skin. He lifted his gaze to Raffaele's face. "But I want you to reduce my salary. I want to earn a pay raise like everyone else does. I don't want people to say that I get paid more because I sleep with the boss."

Raffaele's lips pressed together. "No one will dare say anything."

Nate laughed. "Not about you or to you. People who hate you will keep hating you, and people who admire you won't think less of you just because you fuck an employee. But me? I'm fair game. It was easy enough to hide that we were having sex while I was your PA—I was always with you and no one dared to enter your office without knocking. But it'll be impossible to hide it when I work in a completely different department. People are already talking, Raffaele. And it'll only get worse. Everyone will soon be saying that I'm your fucktoy, and if they find out about my salary, they'll—"

"You're not my fucktoy," Raffaele said, exuding irritation.

Nate smiled. "But that's what people will be saying. Everyone knows you don't do relationships—"

"It's a non-issue." Raffaele laid a hand on Nate's nape and sucked on his bottom lip. "All I'll have to do is change my Facebook relationship status. And it'll take five minutes for the entire company to know."

That was... That was actually a pretty good solution. Being in a serious relationship with the boss would still raise people's eyebrows, but it would be nowhere near as harmful to his professional reputation as being the boss's fucktoy. But wait...

"Isn't fraternization forbidden in the company?" Nate murmured.

"Only within the same department." Raffaele lifted Nate's leg and, hooking it over his hip, slowly slid his cock back into him.

Nate gasped, his eyes slipping shut again. He was just as hard as Raffaele was. Already. Fuck, he hadn't missed his nymphomaniac tendencies around this man. His hole was already eager for more despite being a little sore. He couldn't get enough of this intoxicating feeling—of having Raffaele's cock inside of him, thick and perfect. Sometimes it still took him aback, how much he loved being fucked by this man.

Something about being taken by him was incredibly, toe-curlingly satisfying. He couldn't imagine doing this with another man. But with Raffaele, he couldn't get enough of this.

"It doesn't matter anyway," Raffaele said, his dark eyes a little unfocused as he slowly pumped in and out of him. "I'm the boss. I make the rules."

Groaning, Nate buried his face against Raffaele's shoulder. "Fuck, why is your arrogance so hot?"

Raffaele just laughed and proceeded to fuck his brains out.

Much later, as they lay tangled, exhausted, and sated after round two, Nate had almost drifted off when he felt lips against his ear and heard a quiet, "We can try to hide our relationship if you prefer that."

Nate forced his eyes open. "What do you mean?" he mumbled, his cheek still pressed against Raffaele's chest.

"I don't want to put you into an awkward position," Raffaele said. His voice was steady, but there was a certain reluctance to it that Nate didn't miss.

"You hate the idea of hiding," Nate stated, more curious and surprised than anything else. He had thought that given the choice, Raffaele would prefer to keep quiet about their relationship. He'd avoided relationships for years.

Raffaele didn't say anything for a while, his strong hand stroking Nate's back, up and down. Nate was nearly purring from how good it felt.

"Yes," he confirmed at last, his voice slow as if he was just realizing it. "I'm not used to it."

Nate snorted softly. "You're just used to getting your own way. Hiding would mean that you care about other people's opinions."

"That too," Raffaele said dryly. "But I want everyone to know that you're mine, especially all those besotted idiots in your department."

Nate laughed a little, kissing him on the chest. "You're exaggerating. They're just being nice to me."

"They stare at you all the time and all but drool. It's disgusting."

Nate smiled.

He couldn't deny he was pleased. Of course he wanted Raffaele to think he was attractive, but…

"I'm not that attractive. There are better-looking people out there."

"I don't mean your looks."

"Then what do you mean?" Nate said, propping himself up on his elbow.

Raffaele looked at him through heavy-lidded eyes. "You're... earnest," he said, brushing his thumb over Nate's cheek. "Genuinely friendly and nice. Warm. People are drawn to you. I don't like the way they look at you."

Grinning, Nate leaned down and kissed him softly. "The way they look at me? Just admit you have a jealousy problem."

"I don't have a jealousy problem. I have eyes."

Chuckling, Nate rolled his eyes. "Yeah, you totally don't have a jealousy problem. Maybe you should put a collar on me with your name on it."

"Hm."

"That wasn't a serious suggestion, by the way. Don't get ideas." Dropping his grin, Nate became serious. "I don't want to hide, either. I know there will be people who'll gossip about me behind my back and say nasty stuff. I'm not saying it doesn't bother me at all, but it's not that important, you know?" He gave a small smile. "Frankly, I'm not good at giving a damn about anything or anyone else when it comes to you. That kind of tunnel vision is... it freaks me out, to be honest." Nate blushed a little under Raffaele's gaze. "I've never had it so bad for anyone. It's kind of terrifying and—and you didn't even say the words!"

"What words?"

Nate glowered at him.

Although his face remained blank, Raffaele's eyes were glimmering with amusement.

Then, his lips twitched, before a smile spread over his face.

"Ugh, I hate you," Nate grumbled, hoping his expression wasn't as besotted as he felt. God, he wanted to kiss that smile off his face. How could a man be so arrogant, maddeningly superior, and maddeningly sexy?

"C'mere," Raffaele said. "Give me a kiss."

Nate gave him a kiss.

And then another, and another, because he couldn't help himself.

When they finally parted to get some air into their lungs, Nate's lips felt swollen and oversensitive, his mind hazy and his body warm. He was lying on his back under Raffaele now—he wasn't even sure when they had swapped positions.

Raffaele pressed their foreheads together, his warm breath brushing against Nate's sensitive lips. "Pack your things."

"Hm?" Nate said, his mind still blissfully blank.

"You're moving in with me."

Nate almost laughed. "That's—don't you think it's a little too fast? Especially for a man who didn't do relationships until today."

Raffaele cradled his face with his hands and kissed him again, as if he still couldn't get enough of him. God, Nate could relate.

"It makes sense," Raffaele said, looking at him steadily. "You know the hours I work. If I can't have you with me at work, I want to have you in my home. A few stolen minutes a day isn't enough."

Nate's heart skipped a beat, warmth spreading through his body. The underlying need in Raffaele's words made him feel like he might not be the only one who had it so bad. But he still needed the words.

"I think it's a little early for that," he said, squashing down the almost violent urge to agree. "I still haven't heard the L word," Nate added with a smile, threading his fingers through Raffaele's hair.

Say you love me, say you love me. The strength of that need was kind of disturbing, but he just wanted to hear it, so fucking badly. Although Raffaele had implied that he loved him, hearing him actually say the words was a completely different thing.

"I..." Raffaele looked at him for a moment, his throat working.

And then he said, his voice somehow rough and soft at the same time, "Ti amo."

Oh.

Until now, Nate honestly wouldn't have been able to answer if someone asked him how to say "I love you" in Italian. But looking in Raffaele's dark eyes, it felt like he'd been waiting for them.

Ti amo. The words curled around his heart and warmed him up from the inside. Italian was such a beautiful language.

"You cheat," Nate said with a smile, blinking away the sudden mistiness and kissing the dimple on Raffaele's chin. "You still didn't say the L word!"

Raffaele huffed, a wide smile stretching his lips and making him look ten years younger. "It's not my fault it sounds awkward in English."

Nate looped his arms around his neck. "I guess you'll just have to practice, then," he said, kissing the corner of his mouth and smiling like an idiot. *Ti amo. I love you.* He pushed Raffaele onto his back and arranged them to his satisfaction.

"Let's sleep. I have to get up early tomorrow. Jordan hates tardiness. He's a pretty demanding boss, though compared to you he's soft. You were the devil personified. I probably need to thank you for toughening me up, you dick."

Chuckling, Raffaele slapped him lightly on the ass. "I'm still your boss."

"Oh, I'm sorry, do you want me to call you Sir in bed, too?"

The devilish glint in Raffaele's eyes made Nate's grin fade.

He cleared his throat. "It was just a joke," he said.

"Was it?" Raffaele said mildly, his lips curling into that infuriating little smirk that Nate absolutely had to wipe away with his mouth.

So he did.

There was no more talking for the rest of the night.

Chapter 29

When Nate walked into the office the next morning, no one seemed to be working.

"What's up?" he said, looking in bemusement at all the people gathered around Alex's computer.

"The boss changed his relationship status on Facebook!" Alex said.

Nate tried not to show any outward reaction. Although Raffaele had said he would do it, he hadn't expected that he'd bother doing it so soon. But then again, he wasn't sure why it surprised him. Raffaele wasn't one to hesitate or change his mind once he chose a course of action.

Fuck, Nate missed him already. At his own insistence, they'd arrived at work separately. Nate hadn't seen him ever since Raffaele kissed him goodbye very early in the morning and then left before Nate even properly woke up.

"Do you have any idea who the lucky woman is?" Camilla said.

Someone in the crowd snorted and said, "You mean the unlucky woman?"

"I wish I were that unlucky," Camilla said, rolling her eyes. "He's filthy rich and very hot. So what if he's an asshole? All men are; some are just better at pretending that they aren't."

"Hey, I resent that," Nate said.

"Me, too!" Alex chimed in, laughing. "You're too young to be so cynical."

"You both are exceptions to the rule," Camilla said before peering at Nate. "You were his PA for ages. Surely you have some idea who she might be?"

Nate fidgeted under the scrutiny of twenty pairs of eyes, feeling painfully awkward and unsure. Despite his words to Raffaele last night, he couldn't just say it. He still didn't want to hide, but... away from Raffaele, it was so much harder not to give a damn about his co-workers' opinions.

Fuck, how was he even supposed to reveal that? *Surprise, it's me?*

"What's going on here?" Jordan's sharp voice said from behind. "Why are you not working?"

Everyone quickly returned to their desks, and Nate breathed out. He had never been happier to hear Jordan's voice. But he knew it was just a temporary respite.

The day seemed to drag.

He pretended to be incredibly busy every time his co-workers attempted to question him, putting off the inevitable. He didn't want to lie to anyone, but he had no clue how to tell the truth. Maya had taken the news well—after making fun of him for his inability to keep it in his pants, of course—but his colleagues were an entirely different thing. Nate hadn't expected how big of a deal Raffaele's relationship status would be. The whole building was buzzing with gossip. Just as Raffaele had predicted, it had taken a total of five minutes for the entire company to know about it. There were actually betting pools on who it was. Some supermodel Raffaele had been seen with in the past was currently the favorite.

It irked Nate, his stomach churning with ugly, vicious possessiveness. *He's mine, not hers*, he wanted to snap. *Mine*.

But he didn't know how to say it.

To make things worse, he missed Raffaele already. Despite being in the same building, they might as well be across the city.

Nate couldn't believe how clingy he felt, considering that they'd had sex three times last night. He should have felt sated. And he was—physically. He didn't even necessarily want sex. He just wanted to see him, kiss him, touch him, breathe in Raffaele's scent, and feel his wry smile against his mouth.

God, he had it so bad it was kind of embarrassing. Nate found himself grinning stupidly at random moments. Despite being stressed over how to reveal their relationship to his co-workers, he'd never felt so happy.

Raffaele loved him.

Loved him.

Nate wanted everyone to know that.

He did.

Heck, he wanted to *shout* about it.

But it was so much more difficult to tell the truth now that the rumor mill was running rampant and everyone was incredibly invested in their favorite candidates. He felt like the window of opportunity was gone, and it would just be weird if he said anything now.

Fuck, what a mess.

"Come on, Nate, just give me a hint!" Camilla said. "Is it Karen Milson? The actress? I'm going to bet on her. She accompanied the boss to the anniversary party in honor of the partnership with Rutledge Enterprises. They look so good together."

Nate fixed his gaze on his computer screen. "It was just a publicity stunt for her sake. She's something of an old acquaintance, as far as I know."

Camilla deflated. "Fuck. I'm out of ideas, then. And here I was hoping to sweep the betting pool. I could use the money. Emma wants to go to Disneyland for her birthday, but..."

Nate shot her a sympathetic look. Camilla had become a single mother at nineteen, after her boyfriend had dumped her when he found out about her pregnancy, which was probably why she was so cynical about men. Nate admired her for managing to finish school despite having a baby to take care of. He knew she still struggled financially. Although she was too proud to talk about it much, it was obvious that money was always tight.

He wished he could help her.

But then again... he *could*, couldn't he?

A mischievous smile appeared on his face at the idea. Maybe he could make one person happy when it was revealed who the "secret girlfriend" was.

When it was six o'clock, Nate got to his feet, leaned down to Camilla's ear, and murmured, "Bet on me."

"What?" Camilla said, blinking at him.

Nate just gave her a sheepish smile and a shrug.

Her eyes widened almost comically. "WHAT?"

"Hush," Nate said, glancing around. "Keep it quiet if you want to win."

He walked away quickly, ignoring Camila whisper-yelling at him and demanding answers. It was six already. His workday was over. He couldn't stand the idea of staying here even a moment longer, surrounded by his gossiping colleagues while they speculated about which supermodel *his* Raffaele was in a relationship with.

He would go to Raffaele's apartment and wait for him there. He knew he'd have to wait a long time—Raffaele rarely left work before eight—but Nate didn't care. He wanted to see him. It had been twelve whole hours since he'd seen him. Yeah, "clingy" didn't even begin to describe it, but he didn't give a damn.

Nate was heading across the parking lot to his car when a familiar white Maserati rolled smoothly to a stop in front of him.

Nate stared.

He hadn't expected that Raffaele would want to go home so early—it was so unlike him—but maybe he was just as impatient as Nate was.

The passenger door opened, and Nate smiled helplessly. His feet moved.

The next thing he knew, he was inside the car and then Raffaele was right there, and their mouths were meeting hungrily, licking into each other, pressing closer, tighter. God, this man.

Very distantly, Nate was aware of some noise in the background, but he couldn't focus on anything but Raffaele's arms around him and his firm, sensual lips on his.

When someone wolf-whistled, they broke apart, gasping for air.

Blinking dazedly, Nate opened his eyes.

He found a few dozen people staring at them, their mouths agape, expressions of utter surprise and shock on their faces. A few people had their phones out, clearly taking pictures. Fuck.

A laugh left Nate's mouth. And here he had been, stressing about how to tell his colleagues that they were together.

His face very warm, he looked at Raffaele and just laughed harder when he saw that he was actually attempting to put on his *I'm-your-scary-and-horrible-boss* look. It wasn't working very well, considering that his hair was tousled, his dark eyes were glazed, and his lips were still wet and shiny. He looked infinitely kissable and hot, not scary at all.

The intimidating air was also probably ruined by the fact Nate was practically in his lap.

Nate sat back in the passenger seat and gave an awkward smile to their captive audience just as Raffaele smoothly drove them away. His smile turned sheepish when he noticed Brenda among the gawking crowd. She was the only person who didn't look all that surprised. She gave him a crooked smile and mouthed something that looked suspiciously like *I told you.*

He chuckled, remembering all the times Brenda had tried to convince him that Raffaele treated him differently from everyone else.

"I hope Camilla managed to put a bet on me," Nate mumbled, looking away. The cat was out of the bag now. It was almost a relief. Everyone would know now. And maybe the way it was revealed was for the best, no matter how embarrassing it was. The fact that Raffaele had picked him up—and kissed him—in front of everyone showed that he wasn't ashamed of their relationship—that he was *serious* about Nate. Raffaele wasn't exactly known for public displays of affection.

"What?" Raffaele said, his gaze on the road.

Ignoring his buzzing phone—those were probably messages from his freaking-out co-workers—Nate stared at Raffaele's strong, handsome profile and smiled helplessly. He still couldn't believe this man really was his.

Raffaele loved him. He loved him.

"Nothing," he said, taking Raffaele's free hand. He felt terribly lovesick and clingy, even though Raffaele was right there. Fuck, he wanted to kiss him so badly, but he was driving.

Raffaele glanced at their joined hands. "Don't get soppy on me," he said. But he didn't pull his hand away, and the look in his dark eyes was soft and indulgent.

Nate smiled wistfully, remembering their first meeting. So much had changed in a year. Who could have thought back then that he'd fall in love with that insufferable, seemingly heartless asshole?

"Soppy? Of course not," Nate said with a grin—and intertwined their fingers.

Raffaele rolled his eyes but let him.

The End

Just a Bit Bossy

About the Author

Alessandra Hazard is the author of the bestselling MM romance series *Straight Guys*, *The Wrong Alpha*, *Calluvia's Royalty*.

Visit Alessandra's website to learn more about her books: http://www.alessandrahazard.com/books/

To be notified when Alessandra's new books become available, you can subscribe to her mailing list: http://www.alessandrahazard.com/subscribe/

You can contact the author at her website or email her at author@alessandrahazard.com.

Printed in Great Britain
by Amazon